Praise for *The Best Small Fictions*

"*The Best Small Fictions* . . . could be at the forefront of a burgeoning cultural movement."
— *The Newtown Review of Books*

"It will be well worth your while to spend a minute or 60 with some of the brightest concise writing available today."
— *NewPages*

"The best of these fictional vignettes are like a splash of ice water in the face. Wake up, they shout, your life is unspooling. They create their emotional effects with a quick windup and a powerful release, often a final, lingering image."
— *Harvard Review*

"In this extraordinary collection of small fictions . . . readers are gifted with stories that slap wings onto their backs or drop anchors into their hearts, oftentimes both."
— *The Small Press Book Review*

"[T]he beauty of an anthology such as this, pulling together the best of the form, is that you will always encounter something new, something different, something that pushes the boundaries of flash further than before. If this anthology proves nothing else, it is that small fiction in all its forms continues to go from strength to strength, as does the series itself."
— *Bath Flash Fiction Award*

The Best Small Fictions 2017

The Best Small Fictions

2017

Guest Editor
Amy Hempel

Series Editor
Tara L. Masih

BRADDOCK
AVENUE
BOOKS
UNCOMMON BOOKS · UNCOMMON READERS

For Braddock Avenue Books

2017 Consulting Editors
Leesa Cross-Smith
Ioanna Mavrou
Ben White
Kim Chinquee, Prose Poetry

General Advisory Board
Michael Cocchiarale
Kathy Fish
X. J. Kennedy
Pamela Painter
Robert Shapard
Mary M. Slechta
James Thomas
Clare MacQueen, haibun story and tanka prose

Mel Bosworth, Asst. Ed., Domestic
Michelle Elvy, Asst. Ed., International

Printed in the United States of America
10 9 8 7 6 5 4 3 2 1

FIRST EDITION, September 2017

ISBN 10: 0-998-96671-7
ISBN 13: 978-0-998-96671-7

Cover design by Karen Antonelli
Interior design by Savannah Adams

Braddock Avenue Books
P.O. Box 502
Braddock, PA 15104

www.braddockavenuebooks.com

Braddock Avenue Books is distributed by Small Press Distribution.

For Lalit K. Masih
(1932–2016)
Scholar, artist, philosopher, teacher, father

and

Brian Doyle
(1956–2017)
"There is a story in every thing, and every being,
and every moment, were we alert to catch it, were
we ready with our tender nets . . ."
—from Doyle's
*The Adventures of John Carson in
Several Quarters of the World*

Contents

Foreword

In the preface to his most recent collection, *Fits of Concision: collected poems of six or fewer lines*, award-winning poet X. J. Kennedy writes in defense of brevity: "There's something about [an extremely short poem] that calls for attention. Surrounded by white space, it stands out, glowing like an island inviting us to land. It asks for only a moment of our time, and offers the hope of instant reward."

This is the third volume in *The Best Small Fictions* series. This year we received more nominations, our staff grew, and we moved to a new publisher, Braddock Avenue Books. And this year we are in unprecedented territory politically. Needless to say, getting the 2017 volume together has taken a lot of work under both personal and professional pressure.

But we did it! We are back again (some may not realize we were almost gone), rescued by the wonderful publishers at Braddock, and with the help of a very dedicated, mostly volunteer staff.

What struck me this year in reading over the thousands of prose poems, flashes, micros, haibuns, and so on, was how collectively similar we really are. Despite the variety of styles, formats, scenes, and unique details, many small fictions repeated, explored, and used the same images or themes. Facebook shadowed the 2016 literary world, the election and immigration crept into our creative dialog, dystopian topics and magical realism increased, and I cannot tell you how many stories included coyotes, mannequins, trees, and birds. *Birds,*

birds, birds. We did not see so many birds if any in 2014 or 2015. So what is it about this year that brought so many birds into the stories? While you see examples of these bird-themed fictions in this volume, a great deal more came in. Perhaps almost 60 percent of the nominations included birds. That's a lot of birds.

Perhaps they reflect some prescient Hitchcockian malaise that was forming collectively (see Karen Brennan's "10 Birds," in which birds symbolize dread). In any case, we offer you the best of the ones that feature these little dinosaurs. You have fun contemplating why so many.

Birthing, planning, developing, designing *The Best Small Fictions* has been one of the best experiences of my life. I've been able to work with amazing people both within the covers and without. I've learned a great deal about the state of flash and hybrid fiction (Clare MacQueen and I feel we had a little to do with shining a light on the haibun story), and there is nothing like being able to tell a writer that her or his hard work paid off.

However, it's time for me to hand over the reins. I will remain on as consulting editor, but a new series editor will be taking over for 2018. It's with great pleasure that I turn the series over first to Sherrie Flick. I cannot think of a better person to take it from here. Her professionalism, knowledge of publishing both as one of our most talented flash writers and as an editor, make her the perfect choice. I'm grateful she accepted, and excited to see where she takes the series. Thank you, Sherrie, for your enthusiasm and support.

Thank you also to Jeffrey Condran and Robert Peluso, copublishers at Braddock. We all should thank them. They saved this project from going under, and provide an excellent home and wider distribution. Karen Antonelli had the difficult challenge of creating a new cover that reflected Braddock's brand but also exemplified the series; her retro-contemporary billboard melded both past and present. The talented Savannah Adams provided a wonderful interior design. Our experienced assistant editors, Mel Bosworth and Michelle Elvy, had a huge part in making this series a continued success. The roving editors, Blake Kimzey, Alan King, and Kathryn Kulpa, found some wonderful, overlooked fictions that made it into this volume or onto the finalist list, and our perceptive, skilled consulting editors, Kim Chinquee, Leesa Cross-Smith, Ioanna Mavrou, and Ben White, played a large role in shaping this anthology. We are grateful to our advisory board, especially Mary Slechta and Clare MacQueen, who were consulted this year. Thank you all for your hard work.

But most of our thanks go to esteemed guest editor Amy Hempel for gracing us with her presence, support, time, humor, and expertise in winnowing down 105 finalists to 55 winning small fictions that "glow like islands and allow us to land" for a brief time. Promoting freedom of expression, and the different views that can be explored within story, has never been more of a necessity. These fictions take only a few moments to read, but we promise you will be enlightened, touched, humored, and rewarded.

— Tara L. Masih

Introduction

My favorite definition of a short-short story is that it is "like most ordinary short stories, *only more so.*" This quote is from Irving Howe in his introduction to *Short Shorts*, an anthology published back in the 1960s. These brief stories "cut to the chase," says David Shields in the 2014 anthology, *Life Is Short—Art Is Shorter.*

There is no writing *toward* the story in a short-short; the author must *begin* with the story. From this anthology: "Grandmother kept a diver's knife strapped to her thigh" ("The Sea Urchin"). "One time when I was seven years old, my aunt placed her hands upon me and tried to drive out my devils" ("My Devils"). "You told me not to play with matches that summer, so I palmed a corner-store lighter instead" ("Lottery Days"). Youthful logic—a mind skewed just right or left of center—I don't tire of this. Here is the opening of "Election Cycle": "The circus comes crashing through the wall of your home, all tents and stripes and ballot slips like peanut shells scattered on fine white tile." We then get the whole of an election circus in just 240 words.

And one of the great tests of the success of a short-short story is, of course, the way it ends. Howe said, "This conclusion need not complete the action; it has only to break it off decisively." Shields says the ending "should provide 'retroactive redefinition'—that is, it should force the reader to process anew what she has just read." Punchline or afterthought, it can stake a claim.

The stories selected for this year's *Best Small Fictions* display a range of territory, language, strategy, and effects. They conjure and seduce, they startle and haunt, they are funny and searing, short and shorter. In a recent issue of *Harper's Magazine*, in a piece titled "In Short," poet and essayist Sarah Manguso says about the aphorism, an even shorter form, something that holds for these under-1,000-word stories, too: "The shortest pieces of writing strive not for greatness but perfection (*per*, 'completely,' + *facere*, 'make, do'), the utmost condition of madeness."

Some of the small fictions collected here are aphoristic, some have the shape and application of a modern fable or parable. Others find their footing with a joke, while in others the action is the language itself. There are stories that revolve around a moment in childhood that follows a character throughout a lifetime. There is shame and celebration and reckoning and even epiphany. There are close calls, and partings. There is joy, and there is Joy—I am thrilled to point to the two stories by the incomparable Joy Williams: both "Dearest" and "Polyurethane" are featured in her acclaimed collection *Ninety-Nine Stories of God* (see the spotlight interview with her at the end of this volume).

There is an ekphrastic haibun, a mystery "flash," and stories in the form of lists. There is a meditation on Red Riding Hood. There are fever dreams. The writers come from the West Indies and New Zealand, from Canada, England, Germany, and Japan, in addition to the United States.

Small fictions continue to grow in popularity and impact. There are 55 fresh points of entry in the winning stories here.

— Amy Hempel

The Best Small Fictions 2017

Joy Williams :

36

[From *Ninety-Nine Stories of God* (Tin House Books, 2016)]

Penny had never liked the house and spent as much time as she could away from it. It fit her husband perfectly, however. He loved the open rooms, the little plunge pool beneath the palm trees, the shelves he had built for his many books, the long table where he and his friends played anagrams and poker. When he died, she accepted a position at a university a considerable distance away and rented out the house.

The new tenants adored it. They paid the rent promptly, planted flowers, and befriended the neighbors far more than Penny ever had. In front of the house they parked their three glorious vehicles—a Harley-Davidson, a Porsche, and a white Toyota Tundra.

They wanted to buy but offered a meager price. Penny's price was fair, everyone said so, but the tenants mentioned the roof, the chipped clawfoot tub, the ailing mahogany tree that would have to be taken down, the foundation. There was frequent mention of the foundation. As well, they spoke of the risk they would be taking—the possibility of hurricanes and dengue fever, the continuing poor economy. But they adored the house. This was where they wanted to be.

1

Penny found them irritating in any number of ways—they were ostentatious, full of self-regard, and cheap. They also did not read. But she knew herself well enough to know that they irritated her because they had found happiness in a simple place where she had not.

A few weeks before their lease was up, they offered to meet her price, but she refused them.

After canceling the insurance, she returned to the vacated house. The rooms were immaculate. Even the glass in the windows sparkled. She went from room to room with a clump of sweet and smoldering sage. She tried to think in the language of blessing. Then, with the assistance of a few gallons of accelerant, she set all that had been the structure on fire.

DEAREST

Joy Williams :

82

[From *Ninety-Nine Stories of God* (Tin House Books, 2016)]

She liked traveling through the American southwest and staying in the rooms of old hotels in forgotten towns. The questionable cleanliness of the rooms did not bother her nor did the indifferent food served at erratic times in the local cafés. She went to markets and churches, bought trinkets and the occasional rug. She never had any real experiences but she was content. This was how she spent her monthlong vacation year after year. She was a teacher of history and mathematics, though not a particularly dedicated one. She moved them along, the little ones.

One evening, in a particularly garish room of awkward dimensions, jammed with oak furniture, with prints of long-ago parades covering the walls, she experienced an un-familiar unease.

She decided to remove the few articles of clothing she had earlier placed in the bureau drawer and return them to her valise. This gave her the feeling she would soon be on her way again. Removing the cargo pants with the touch of spandex to add stretch and the linen shirt with hidden button-front plackets, she noticed writing in the bottom of the drawer.

Under the sensible beam of the flashlight she always carried, she read.

On the displacement and destruction of the American Indian, George Caitlin wrote in 1837:

For the nation there is an unrequited amount of sin and injustice that sooner or later will call for national retribution. For the American citizens who live, everywhere proud of their growing wealth and their luxuries, over the bones of these poor fellows, there is a lingering terror for reflecting minds: Our mortal bodies must soon take their humble places with their red brethren under the same glebe; to appear and stand at last, with guilt's shivering conviction, among the myriad ranks of accusing spirits at the final day of resurrection.

She closed the drawer and immediately vowed to no longer frequent public accommodations. She would purchase a mobile home and continue her travels unharried by the sentiments of others. But, she had no idea who this person was now who would continue.

POLYURETHANE

Joy Williams is the acclaimed author of five collections of stories including, most recently, *Ninety-Nine Stories of God*, and *The Visiting Privilege*, winner of the PEN/Malamud Award. She has also published four novels, including *The Quick and the Dead*, which was a finalist for the Pulitzer Prize, and a book of essays, *Ill Nature*, which was a finalist for the National Book Critics Circle Award. Among her many honors are the Rea Award for the short story and the Strauss Living Award from the American Academy of Arts and Letters. She has taught at the Universities of Houston, Florida, Iowa, and Arizona.

Larry Brown :

Triangle

[From *SAND Journal*, Issue 14, 2016]

Blue triangles, solid blue. Too blue, almost, for a food. She brought the cereal with her from her mother's. On the box, blue triangles rain from the sky, landing and glistening in a glass bowl. She is the reason I buy milk.

I set my beer on the counter. A light beer, as if it makes any difference now. My cell hangs at my hip, new Reveille ringtone uploaded. I am considering growing a goatee.

That's your dinner? I say.

She scoops more blue triangles from the bowl and slants the spoon across to where her chin rests in her palm, elbow pinning the notebook open on the table. Perched atop her head are dollar-store reading glasses. Her eyes are fine. This must be fashion.

So, she says, not looking up, that's your dinner?

I am about to take a drink.

Joking, she says.

Really, she says. She adjusts the glasses on her head, glances my way.

I get it, I say. The floor creaks, my weight shifting. I am smiling.

Larry Brown :

I go to the living room, close the venetian blinds, flick on a couple lamps, check my cell, knowing I missed nothing but believing I could have. Back to the kitchen and my spot at the counter, thinking I should have upped the thermostat, thinking a goatee, well, it could look, I don't know, forced.

Sometimes I forget, I say. The lights, I forget they're on.

She lifts her elbow and the notebook page flips on its own.

If I remember, if I'm in bed, I say, coming back downstairs feels too far to go.

The fridge hums. My beer seems to be emptying itself.

I shrug. Sorry, I know you're studying. *Trifling*. Her word, earlier, to describe the math test tomorrow.

Those lights, they're like a night light for you, she says. Nothing wrong with that.

Night light? I say. Then, softer, I add, Maybe.

She pushes away from the table. She dumps her bowl into the sink, wipes her hands on the dishtowel. Triangles, not such a solid blue anymore, crowd the drain.

Dad, she says.

Then she springs, her arms locking over mine, trapping my arms to my body. I hear a gasp. It's me. She places her head against my shoulder.

You're not so fast, she says, continuing the hug.

Reading glasses stare up at me. I shake my head.

I can't slow down, I say.

Larry Brown lives in Brantford, Ontario. He is the author of the story collection *Talk* (Oberon Press, 2009) and recently completed his second collection, which mixes flash fiction and longer stories, titled *Satellite*. His stories have also appeared in *The Antigonish Review, The New Quarterly, The Fiddlehead, The Malahat Review,* and other literary magazines in Canada. Brown studied fiction writing at the University of Iowa's Summer Writing Workshop and the Humber College School for Writers, and teaches writing workshops across Ontario.

Len Kuntz :
Summer Scalping: Scarecrows

[From *I'm Not Supposed to Be Here and Neither Are You*
(Unknown Press, 2016)]

Mother teaches us how to steal.

We start with Henderson's corn field, undercover of the night, our station wagon skulking down the dusty aisle ends like a muttering alligator. She throws us out, tosses us the gunnies and we scamper through the rows and I start ripping off ears as fast as I can. It feels like cheap murder or beating up a kid, someone helpless and smaller than me. When I pull them from the stalk, they make a scratching noise similar to Mother's fingernails on the arm rest or the sketchy rumble of her cigarette cough. The corn leaves are ridged and sweaty and the corn hair tickles my neck, but just for a moment until Davey jams his elbow into my rib.

"Stop fucking around," he says. His eyes are electric brown, Mexican jumping beans. Black smears of grease sit below them. Davey takes this shit seriously. He looks like a resentful quarterback or a warrior looking for a scalp.

When I still don't get it, he slugs me in the gut. "Don't be stupid. We work in the middle."

He hisses, flops down and slides in the dirt on his belly, an iguana now, a combat soldier. He motions that I should follow and I do because I am scared and confused and dizzy. Old Man Henderson is who we work for during the day, and here we are robbing him at night. I know these fields as well as I know the twelve-by-twelve bedroom that I share with Davey. We shouldn't be here. We're poor but we're not starving.

In the center of the field the stalks sway with the breeze, their tops tipping and dipping, brushing our shoulders as we work, whispering conspiratorially. I can't stop shivering even though it's a hot, humid summer night.

Davey has a flashlight. One end is stuffed in his mouth. Light comes out the other end in swaths and cones. Davey's face glows menacing lavender. He sees me staring and thwacks me across the forehead with the flashlight. He calls me a stupid fag as I finger the new bruise and rub his saliva from my eye.

I helped Mr. Henderson put up the new set of scarecrows that stand at the sides of the field, arms outstretched as if crucified. It was a lazy job, given to me, I presumed, as a kindly favor. Usually I was charged with moving the twenty-foot-long irrigation pipes and shoring up rows or pruning, which is the same as prison work when the temperature gets past a hundred. Anyway, Mrs. Henderson gave him half a dozen Albertson grocery bags stuffed with all sorts of clothing articles and Mr. Henderson said, "Go to it." As a test run for bringing up the news to Mother, I'd once confessed to Mr. Henderson that I wanted to be a fashion designer when I grew up. His eyes worked over my statement and out of his shirt pocket he pulled a piece of straw the size of a pencil. He chewed it for a while. It took him so long to answer that I thought my shame might burn me to death, but then he showed me a grin. It was wide and toothy and real. "That's wonderful, son." No one had ever called me that. "It's important to have large-sized dreams." So

9

I figured there was a tie to me confiding in Mr. Henderson that day and him wanting me to put together a collection of scarecrows. I did as I was told. I would have, no matter the request, since I was getting paid cash money and, as anybody can tell you, that's a hard thing to come by. When I was finished I had six fairly realistic men. They were skinny things because the straw kept slipping down their drawers or out of their sleeves. But they looked fine, stylish even. Afterward there were a few garments left over, one being a sky blue turtleneck that didn't make sense on a scarecrow. Mr. Henderson said, "You like it?" I lied and said, "No," because even though the color was blue, it was too light, pastel, bordering on effeminate, and I didn't want him or anyone else getting ideas. "Take it," he said. "Go on." And I did. After I got home, I stuck it between the box springs and the mattress I share with Davey. One of these days I plan on showing him, but that might not be for a while.

When our gunny sacks are full of corn we stagger in the dark toward the lurking station wagon. Mother sits smoking with the dome light on. She doesn't blink, doesn't say a word, just starts the engine and pulls the silver stick shift on the side of the steering wheel and we drive off.

The next morning Mr. Henderson calls me to his office, which is a trailer sunk into the sun-baked mud northeast of where some broke-down combines slumber. His golden lab, Leroy, scents me, sneezes, and scampers off. A crow caws.

He shouts to come on in when I knock. I hesitate and try to measure the tone of his voice, sift through it like a gold miner, for evidence of a mood. The door catches and won't open. "Kick it at the bottom!" he tells me. I wonder why he doesn't just open the thing for me.

"You gotta kick it!" he says. I still can't tell if there's anything to learn from his tone, but by now I'm running and his voice isn't very loud. Stalks slap me because I'm off balance. My feet burn, my eyes sting. It's not even noon yet. I sweat. I run through the corn row and don't stop.

Len Kuntz is a writer from Washington State, an editor at the online magazine *Literary Orphans*, and the author of *I'm Not Supposed to Be Here and Neither Are You* (Unknown Press, 2016). Over 1,000 of his stories and/or poems have appeared in literary journals such as *PANK*, *Elimae*, and *Boston Literary Magazine*. He has received multiple nominations for the Pushcart Prize, his stories have been chosen for Best of the Net ten times, and his first story collection, *The Dark Sunshine* (Connotation Press, 2014), was nominated for the Phillip H. McMath Book Award.

Alex Simand :
Election Cycle

[From *Sonic Boom*, Issue 6, 2016]

The circus comes crashing through the wall of your home, all tents and stripes and ballot slips like peanut shells scattered on fine white tile. You never asked for the circus, but it comes anyway. Picket signs. Carrot cakes. Globs of spittle from when your neighbor calls you a communist. A man on a podium puts his head in the mouth of a lion and says, *See? You Can Trust Me.* He smiles for the camera and the lion rolls its eyes. Sometimes the lion bites his head off but he grows another and gesticulates forcefully with his thumbs. The ringleader appears wearing a sequin gown and the calves of a squat thruster. She begs you to believe her but her teeth run away, chattering, from her mouth. A bull-sized pigeon plucks its way on stage and eats a piece of fried chicken, explains that, no, it's not quite cannibalism. The man with the lion mouth around his head is saying something through the gills in his neck. *Don't trust lizard people,* he says. *Don't trust lizard people or anyone with a red crayon in his hand, especially around white walls.* You want it all to stop, the circus, but all your friends keep lining up to buy tickets. Around the block they line up, starving to the ribs for spectacle. You're not sure you have friends anymore. Only audience members. That must make you the clown.

Alex Simand lives and works in San Francisco but grew up in Toronto. Simand writes fiction, creative nonfiction, and poetry. His work has appeared or will appear in *Hippocampus, North American Review, Red Fez, Mudseason Review, FIVE:2:ONE* magazine, *Angel City Review, Drunk Monkeys,* and other publications. Simand is the former blog editor and editor of creative nonfiction for *Lunch Ticket*, as well as for the Diana Woods Memorial Award hosted by *Lunch Ticket*. A contributing writer for *HOOT* and associate editor at Zoetic Press, he holds an MFA from Antioch University–Los Angeles.

Pamela Painter
Help

[From *Five Points*, Issue 17, No. 3]

The music decibel is at an all-time high, and the bar-back just quit. So Benny's pulling beers, pissier than usual. He tells Denise he hates college kids but he hates yuppies more. He gives her the job of sloshing glasses clean on upside-down mops that pass for a dishwasher. The job sucks, but Denise is taking the semester off to save money for art supplies. Benny doesn't know this. As she lowers a glass onto a soapy mop and turns it around, Benny elbows her arm. "I'm timing them," he says, his gaze locked on *Gents*. "The girl went in first and he followed." He pulls another Bud into a cleanish glass. "The girl in the pink skirt?" Denise asks. She feels like she's screaming. "Three minutes, maybe five, they're doing dope," he yells. "Any longer, it's sex. No respect for whoever else has to take a piss." Minutes pass. Denise pictures the girl's pink skirt hiked up, panties tight around her ankles. "Watch this," Benny says, and muscles out from behind the bar, a door wedge in his hand. Denise doesn't have to watch to know where he puts it. He's back and only he and Denise can separate the thumping of the jukebox from fists pounding on the door. "You hear that." Benny grins. She nods. Sadly, she hears it. Once she was locked in a ladies room, something gone wrong with the door. She remembers calling "Somebody?" It sounds stupid to her now, calling "Somebody?" But finally somebody came.

Pamela Painter is the author of four story collections, most recently *Ways to Spend the Night*, and coauthor of the popular textbook *What If? Writing Exercises for Fiction Writers*. Her stories have appeared in *The Atlantic, Five Points, Harper's, Kenyon Review, SmokeLong Quarterly*, and *Ploughshares*, among others, and have been collected in numerous anthologies such as *Sudden Fiction, Flash Fiction,* and *Microfiction*. She received grants from the Massachusetts Artists Foundation and the National Endowment for the Arts, and won three Pushcart Prizes and *Agni Review*'s John Cheever Award for Fiction. Painter's stories have been presented by WordTheatre on stage in London, Los Angeles, and New York. She teaches at Boston's Emerson College.

Allegra Hyde :
Syndication

[From *Of This New World* (University of Iowa Press, 2016)]

My parents are in the backyard, digging their graves. I'm in the kitchen with Orange, my younger brother, and we're watching through a grubby little window. My parents work without speaking. They are not fit people, but they do not stop for breaks. Sweat blooms under their armpits and around their bandanas.

The graves are being dug next to the outhouse, and are approaching six feet by four feet by three feet.

That's how I know they aren't for us.

Still, I decide it would be best to keep Orange from watching, so I suggest we play one of our favorite games: Prank Call! It's where we dial random numbers and pretend to be debt collectors. Sometimes we pretend to be hookers, too. Or long lost children.

Orange wraps his sticky fingers around the phone receiver, forehead pleating into focus. His tongue lolls out of his mouth like a fat pink slug. He's an ugly kid—but he doesn't know that yet—which makes me love him even more.

"Broked." Orange looks at me, confused.

I press the phone against my ear and listen for a dial tone.

"Broked," I echo.

Through the window we hear the dirt-gnaw of shovels: the scrape and thump, scrape and thump.

I know I should be full of fearing, but instead I feel a sense of lightness—a birthday party feeling—like anything could happen and it's my day to choose.

"Put your rain boots on," I tell Orange, even though the sky is clear and it's been the hottest August ever.

Orange doesn't argue. Besides failing to notice his own ugliness, he hasn't yet discovered he's allowed to say no, which is also something I like about him, most of the time.

While Orange gets his rain boots, I hear a new sound: a hush-hush sound. I peer out the kitchen window and see two rectangular holes. Two shovels propped against the outhouse.

I do not see our parents.

Orange comes up beside me, his eyes as wide as soup bowls.

"Look," I say, and point toward two quails tottering across the yard. "Our parents have turned into birds."

I'm joking, of course, but Orange skitters through the kitchen and out the front door, hollering at the quails until they go goosing into the sky.

I run out after him. Now I'm scared, just like the quails, by all the noisiness after quiet. I grab Orange's hand and keep running. The two of us careen across the yard, plunging into the forest that surrounds our house like a leafy overcoat—trees in every direction—except for a single narrow road, like a dirt zipper.

Orange and I crash and bump and skin our knees, and we go from cold-sweat-scared to laugh-leaping and collapsing in a heap of giggles and blood in the mossy nook of a pine tree.

"Hey, you got a light?" says Orange, which is something he must have heard on TV.

I pantomime taking a lighter out of my dress pocket, and then we both smoke imaginary cigars.

"Where can a guy get a drink around here?" murmurs Orange, already half-fallen asleep.

I put a piece of moss under his head. Then I put a piece of moss under my head and close my eyes and imagine both of us being hugged tight and warm by a huge fur coat, its pockets full of cough drops and unused handkerchiefs.

When we wake, the sun has sunk low enough to stab sideways through trees. It's the time of day our parents usually come trundling up the dirt road in their truck and we all sit down in front of the TV and Mom massages Dad's feet and I massage my own feet, and sometimes Orange's feet, until Dad calls me a little perv.

Orange and I both wake up stiff, so we start walking through the woods in no particular direction. I can tell Orange is hungry because I'm hungry, too. Neither of us says anything, though, because we're too busy seeing our parents everywhere. We see a pair of squirrels chattering at us from a tree branch. Then two stumps, mossy and indignant. Two beams of light.

Orange shivers because he's only wearing rain boots and a diaper. He's potty-trained, but he prefers the feel, he says— it's like a butt pillow—and Mom said that was fine because it meant less laundry.

I pull off my dress and give it to him. The dress drags around his ankles, but he's careful not to trip. Now I'm just in my undies and sandals. It makes me feel strong, being mostly naked. I don't feel cold. I give Orange another imaginary cigar.

The last dribbles of daylight leak from the forest, and Orange and I begin bumping into things. The bumping is almost fun, though, and I start to get the birthday party feeling again. I start believing things could go on like this—like it might always be me and my brother on an adventure—like it might always be my day to choose.

Except then we catch sight of a lamp-lit window.

Orange and I slide up to the house like ghosts, or arsonists. Or like two children who've always longed to discover another house out in the woods away from their doomsday-prepping bandana-wearing parents, but who are also nervous now that they've found it. Orange nearly trips on the hem of my dress and makes a squeaking sound. We both freeze, but nothing happens. An open window, square as a TV frame, pours out light. We slip our heads up over the windowsill, chins on the ledge, because at night it's always easier to in-look than out-look.

And we look. We drink in this other life.

After a few minutes, though, I slide my chin off the windowsill. I've realized that I've seen this show before—I know what will happen—and it makes me feel proud and sad at the same time: my knowing.

Orange keeps watching, his big ugly grin lit by the window-glow.

I start massaging his feet. I do this until we both feel a gentle kind of happy.

For now, no one tells me to stop.

Allegra Hyde is the author of the short story collection *Of This New World* (University of Iowa Press, 2016), winner of the John Simmons Short Fiction Award. Her stories and essays have appeared in *The Missouri Review, New England Review, The Gettysburg Review, The Threepenny Review,* and elsewhere. She is the recipient of a Pushcart Prize, as well as support from the Virginia G. Piper Center for Creative Writing, the Jentel Artist Residency Program, the Lucas Artists Residency Program, The Elizabeth George Foundation, and the U.S. Fulbright Commission. She currently lives in Houston, Texas.

Stuart Dybek :
Ascent

[From *Gulf Coast*, Summer/Fall 2016]

They were ascending a staircase that might bring them closer to the mystery. Each shouldered a stair that seemed at first immaterial, but as the ascent continued, its weight could be discerned by the bow of backs and breaths growing shorter as if the air had thinned. When the staircase ended suddenly before an edge overhanging a void, the ascendant knelt and set the stair into place. It fit perfectly as if it had been expected, ready to support the footfalls to follow, its moonlit tread and riser of shadow in perfect uniformity with the spiraling flight of preceding stairs. The task completed, the ascendant stood aside, silently joining hands with the ghostly balustrade of those who had come before and, closing his eyes and fading into a dreamless sleep, allowed the next climbers to pass.

From afar, their climb must have appeared processional: a living current flowing upward at a pace undeterred by accident or conflict, as if ascension was obedient to a law greater than gravity. Bombarded by starlight, the climbers reflected the radiance. Beneath the dome of the universe, they looked barely corporeal. The birthing-dying galaxies shined through them so that their inner lives—their most intimate memories and dreams—were as visible as the organs of a gecko in the glow of a porch light. Across the stillness of black matter, the synchronized stamp of their footfalls, regular as the pulsing of quasars, beat out an elementary measure of time. From a celestial distance the ascent was beautiful.

Like all beauty shaped from chaos, its preservation depended on order. Perhaps that was the law more powerful than gravity. To disturb the order would threaten a return to the emptiness from which the staircase and those who climbed it were, not so much composed, as organized. From a distant perspective it was obvious—whether the ascendants recognized it or not—that when each of them reached the last step and was required to stand aside, the change was merely one of degree rather than of kind.

There were other immutable laws. Possessiveness was forbidden. Whatever an ascendant professed to believe, he or she—not that gender mattered—ultimately possessed nothing. No matter how passionately the ascendants felt themselves possessed, how much they loved or hated, what allegiances they'd formed over the course of their climb, they possessed nothing. In that they were equal. Balanced at the edge, it was not permissible for the ascendant to hug to the stair, refusing to release the weight he'd carried, to which he'd grown attached so that what had once been a burden now seemed a part of him. It was not permitted to raise the stair that had been dutifully transported to that incalculable height—a summit erected by all those who step by step had preceded—and in a final tantrum of rebellion hurl it over the edge before leaping after.

Worse still was the penultimate offense of trying to go back down.

Stuart Dybek is the author of five books of fiction including *Ecstatic Cahoots*, a book of short fictions and prose poems, and also two collections of poetry. In addition, his latest book, *The Start of Something: The Selected Stories of Stuart Dybek*, was published by Jonathan Cape/Vintage in 2016. His work has appeared in *The New Yorker, Harper's, The Atlantic, Poetry,* and *Tin House*. Awards include a PEN/Malamud Prize, fellowships from the NEA and the Guggenheim Foundation, and a John D. and Catherine T. MacArthur Foundation Fellowship. Dybek is currently Distinguished Writer in Residence at Northwestern University.

Kathy Fish :
Strong Tongue

[From *Cheap Pop*, December 2016]

The dentist is attempting to install two crowns on my teeth, but he has to call in reinforcements. *Can you just try to keep your tongue out of the way*, he asks. A man and a young woman come into the room. The woman is normal-sized, but the man's the size of a bull. He doesn't look like a member of the dental profession. Maybe he's just brought in when someone has a very strong tongue. The woman pries my mouth open with some contraption and the bull-sized man clenches my tongue in his gloved hand. *It's like a bucking bronco*, he says. Some of his spit lands on my eyelid.

The snow pile in the middle of the cul-de-sac, once shaped like the Matterhorn, has shrunk and gone sooty. There's a half-eaten sandwich at its base. I kick some snow over it. Supreme the neighbor dog paws it out and eats it.

I call my mother and tell her about the new wrinkle on my forehead, deeper than the others. I tell her about the dentist. All these things are happening to my body. I hear her chewing. *Why do you care?* she says. *You were never that pretty.*

Kathy Fish :

My tongue is strong because I have figured out a trick and it's this: If you press your tongue hard to the roof of your mouth and make a half smile, it makes your neck look younger and firmer. After my dentist appointment, I had driven to King Soopers and sat sobbing in my car. An old guy tapped on the window. He gave me his monogrammed hanky and a lecture on ninety-degree parking.

Supreme the dog belongs to the man across the street. He'd once had a wife, but she died in her sleep soon after they were married. He said for six weeks all he did was drive around eating Taco Bell with the radio blasting. He rescued Supreme from a puppy mill. She'd had so many litters her nipples were raw and hard as pebbles.

My mother says I shouldn't take the new job in the new city. She reminds me how often I get lost. *Even with GPS and that takes some doing*, she says. *Have you forgotten those three months in St. Louis?*

My tongue is strong because I hold it so much.

When I meditate, I listen to Solfeggio tones through my headphones. I have some things to get over and my doctor said it will release my anxiety and open my Third Eye. My doctor isn't a real doctor but she makes me feel better. I lie back and imagine I'm in the dentist chair and they are all telling me how good I am. How I am no trouble at all. Behind my eyelids I see snow and tongues and teeth. I see my own neck, long and smooth as the stem of a daisy.

Kathy Fish's stories have been published and anthologized widely, most recently in *Yemassee Journal, Newfound Journal, New South,* and *Best Small Fictions 2016*. She is the author of three collections: a chapbook in *A Peculiar Feeling of Restlessness: Four Chapbooks of Short Short Fiction by Four Women* (Rose Metal Press, 2008); *Wild Life* (Matter Press, 2011); *Together We Can Bury It* (The Lit Pub, 2012); and she coauthored a flash fiction collection with Robert Vaughan, *Rift* (Unknown Press, 2015). Fish teaches flash fiction for the Mile High MFA program at Regis University in Denver, Colorado.

Marci Calabretta Cancio-Bello

The Sea Urchin

[From *Paper Darts*, January 11, 2016]

Grandmother kept a diver's knife strapped to her thigh. Daily, before the night could fray into dawn, she dived half a mile from shore, inhaling three minutes of air at a time. All morning she pried abalone and sea urchins from slick rock. Once, when she returned, I counted the stiff lines around her mouth, which never seemed to open but held back entire tides. On my birthday, she brought me a ball of spines in a bucket, lifted its bit of ocean into my cupped hands. The creature's round mouth explored the cracks of my palm, tasting the salt on my skin, recoiling. An offering like the pincushions I often brought my mother, every needle threaded with a different color. Grandmother boiled garlic, soybeans, salt into broth, ladled the seaweed soup into a white bowl. She turned the urchin and broke it open, scooped out the ocher roe with a spoon, dropped it in among the kelp. How it sank like a sun into the murk, dissolved. I spooned mouthfuls at a time as she harvested the rest of the body's cavern, a move as practiced as mending her thick black diving skins and nets. Her fingers were steady against the spines. What I remember is not the sweetness or the slickness, but the heat rising from the broth, a mouth wide enough to swallow the needles and flesh of the sea.

Marci Calabretta Cancio-Bello is the author of *Hour of the Ox* (University of Pittsburgh Press, 2016), which won the 2015 AWP Donald Hall Prize and the 2016 Florida Book Awards Bronze Medal for Poetry. She earned a dual BA in English and Creative Writing from Carnegie Mellon University, and an MFA in Creative Writing from Florida International University, where she was awarded the inaugural John S. and James L. Knight Poetry Fellowship and two Academy of American Poets Prizes. She serves as cofounding editor for *Print-Oriented Bastards*, as producer for *The Working Poet Radio Show*, and as a program coordinator for Miami Book Fair International.

Phillip Sterling :
Registry

[From *The Careless Embrace of the Boneshaker* (great
weather for MEDIA, 2016)]

Her dishes were mismatched to begin with. Some of her set was
porcelain, morning glories vining around the edge; some of it
was Corelle. Several china teacups with matching saucers had
been hand-painted with what looked to be pink lady slippers.
One stoneware serving bowl boasted a bright sunflower. Most
of the set had come from yard and rummage sales, the annual
white elephant event at the church, estate auctions, curio
boutiques, or consignment stores. She had collected randomly
at first, what her whimsy begged, or what struck her fancy,
which was, at the onset—as she herself admits—somewhat
scattershot ("scatterbrained" was one lover's parting word),
an aesthetic formed at a moment's spur and feint, at times
reactionary even, given one's companion's pigheadedness.
Yet over time her tastes solidified and she found herself with
dinner plates or soup bowls of a distinctly yellowish-brown
nature, though various tints of olive or mustard were tolerated
as long as flowers were prominent, for flowers were essential
to her collection. At Thanksgiving, her table looked like an
overgrown English garden.

His dishes were mismatched to begin with. He had acquired them from his mother, her old dishes, dishes she was no longer happy with, or sets that were incomplete, with only three salad plates, for example, and a hideous blue and orange casserole dish someone had abandoned at a Cub Scout potluck. His mother had furnished him with dishes she had meant to drop at the Salvation Army years before but had misplaced; she found the box in a closet of the spare room, behind the cedar chest, when she was looking for bedding to send with him to college. During college, as he migrated from dorm to living space to apartment, he lost some of the dishes his mother had given him, lost or broke them (more than half of the glassware, in fact) and so replaced it periodically—at times with the white stoneware he filched from the dining hall, at times with the embossed china of some fancy eating establishment (taken on a dare). At the end, his collection included nine salt shakers, seven for pepper (though one, from the looks of the holes, may have been misused), two cheese mills, and a creamer.

The first time she stayed at his place (she would say, whenever someone asked), she had looked in his cupboard for a teacup and found a Goodwill store. She had laughed. It was something they seemed to have in common. They both laughed.

Now they were talking marriage, or at least moving in together, simplifying, downsizing, combining the households (their fortunes and misfortunes), partnering.

"What do we do about the dishes?" she asked. "I mean, what will it say about us if we pack them up and give them away—return them to Goodwill or something, sell them in the yard? What will it say about us if we register at Macy's for a complete, matching set?"

"Or use them for skeet shooting," the man said, thinking less of his white plates than of her flowery brown ones, brownish birds winging across a pale blue sky. After all, his set was an heirloom of sorts; they'd been with him for years. They held certain memories. He couldn't bring himself to think of smashing them intentionally. Or giving them to strangers. Perhaps his sister's kids, his nieces, now that they approached their teens, would want his dishes, would pack them off to college, add to the collection, start a tradition, make of the dishes a family story.

"Or perhaps," she said, "we could salvage the ones we have the most matches to, the most complete set, add to it from open stock." She was thinking of the porcelain with the morning glories. Hadn't she seen something like that . . . or close enough . . . at Target?

"What's wrong with what we have already?" he said. "It seems silly to spend money on something we don't really need, at least not right away."

He spoke softly, from across the small table, where he sat on a chair that matched the one she was sitting on, though without the floral cushion. He didn't look up from the house-ware catalog that overlapped the plate he'd pushed aside. His coffee mug prevented the page from turning.

"Want anything else?" she asked, rising. She hesitated, briefly, as if she had something more to say, then picked up the saucer she'd used for her egg and set it on the counter. A bit of yolk had already dried on the pattern, like a late yellow bloom caught in early frost. From where she stood, she could see through the window the neighbor's yard, their above-ground pool, which they had used maybe a half-dozen times all summer. It was covered in a black tarp.

"No," he said. "Thanks."

It was October, a Sunday. And while the woman at the sink knew there were things that needed to be done—dishes to wash and put away, a skirt and blouse to set out for the morning, a thank-you note to send to her mother (important things, necessary things)—she could not move. Water from the faucet filled the sink, dumbing its clamor of mismatched dishes. The neighbor's pool looked pathetic. And the old sadness came back to her, familiar and fathomless.

Phillip Sterling is the author of *And Then Snow* (Main Street Rag Press, 2017), *In Which Brief Stories Are Told* (Wayne State University Press, 2011), *Mutual Shores* (New Issue, 2000), and four chapbook-length series of poems. Editor of *Imported Breads: Literature of Cultural Exchange* (Mammoth, 2003) and *Isle Royale from the AIR: Poems, Stories, and Songs from 25 Years of Artists-in-Residence* (Caffeinated Press, 2017), he is a former awardee of two Fulbright Lectureships (Belgium and Poland) and has served as artist-in-residence for the U.S. Park Service at both Isle Royale National Park and Sleeping Bear Dunes National Lakeshore in Michigan.

Nick Almeida :
Watchdog

[From *The Baltimore Review*, Winter Issue, 2016]

Our mother had a tattoo. A blue dog under her shoulder blade, no bigger than the pit of a plum. When she let us, we ran our fingers over it and howled.

She cooped herself in her bedroom for quiet, lights out, hours at a time. We were animals. When he got home from the job site, Pap told us, Shut up. You're making her nuts. Most of the time she hid it, but in summer she let the dog out. We saw it sweat in the sunshine, bound to her back by a bright bra strap. Later, she left for Montana with Neal—the man from the computer, Pap called him—and the dog went, too. In time, we left. Some of us for jobs, or school, or nothing at all. Some of us forgot about our mother and her dog.

Our sister had a tattoo but never showed us. She deployed and our brother forwarded us a video she'd made for Thanksgiving. *Habash.* Arabic for "turkey." When she turned and laughed, there it was. A little dog behind her ear. I imagined that was where a helmet might rest. She turned up later, quieter than our mother had been.

My grandmother had a tattoo. Cleaning out my brother's apartment, I found her photograph pressed in a stack of *Motor Trends.* In the picture, my grandmother has little charcoal eyes. A pinup queen. Shoulders back, a hand wrapped around her neck as if holding it up. The picture is old, but you can still see the little dog on her wrist. Everything else was sold or thrown away.

Some nights, as I lie in bed next to Gloria and feel her breath on my shoulder, I think of dogs. Our daughter sleeps in a crib against the wall. I stay awake for the two of them, listening to my wife sleep, counting our child's breaths, praying everything is as it should be. I tense up at every car horn, every shuffle of feet on the sidewalk outside. Now and then, I look to the door. No one gets in, no one gets out. And in those dark hours between asleep and awake, I think, maybe I am one of those dogs. A dog perched on the slender shoulder of a woman I love. I am a watchdog watching skin, watching silence, watching the permanent ink, watching, so you can't leave, you can't take me away.

Nick Almeida is a graduate of the Michener Center for Writers, where he studied fiction and served as editor-in-chief for *Bat City Review*. He holds an MA from Penn State University. His work has appeared in *Yemassee, Broadsided, The Baltimore Review,* and elsewhere.

Tara Laskowski :
States of Matter

[From *Ellery Queen's Mystery Magazine*, May 2016]

The first time I saw him he was tossing shovels of dirt purpose-fully, steadily. I could see the darkened patches of his shirt, the rounded tightness of his biceps, and I thought, *this is a man who gets things done.* I'd always thought gravediggers were old and creepy, half-dead themselves, but that day in the harsh sun he was nothing if not alive. I'd never dug a grave before, but I'd shoveled snow. It was tough on the back.

Later, on our first date, staring across the sticky table at TGI Fridays, he was quiet, leaving me to fill in all the spaces with my jabbering. He didn't ask why I was in the cemetery that day. To whom I was bringing flowers.

Here's how I imagine it: The gust blew away the little girl's balloon. She followed it, black patent leather shoes stomping through the rough grass on the outskirts of the fall festival. Up, up, past the Ferris wheel, a dot in the sky.

The man with the ponytail was there, then. Perhaps he'd followed her, perhaps he'd always been there. He wiped her tears. The wind bellowed again, kicking up old popcorn bags and dirty napkins, swirling the girl's hair against his shoulder. He offered his hand, looping it around hers.

When the trash settled again in stillness, my sister was gone.

The gravedigger burned his fingers out in the woods. I pressed a cold wet washcloth around them. His eyes pinched. I wondered about blisters.

When I was a kid, they told moms and dads to use butter. How many times had I shoved a throbbing finger in that soft fat yellow, tears plopping off the kitchen counter. Now they say the grease makes it worse, seals in the heat instead.

The plastic cards had burned quicker than the clothes. He kept saying no big deal, like he'd picked up a Happy Meal on the way home. I'd known him for months now, knew not to ask what I wanted to: Had the man shown fear? Did he still have a ponytail? What is the sound of shovel meeting skull?

Back in my apartment, I kissed him. I liked the feel of his calloused hands on my body, the way his muscles tensed and relaxed like a slithering amphibian. In the middle of July everything smoldered. We stood in front of the open window, traffic roaring below, not caring who saw.

The lake was deserted. We could only see when the moon dodged the clouds. Down by the shore, the mud was like clay. Easy digging. One last tiny hole.

We placed the shoes in, patent leather catching the moon like a wink. I didn't watch as he covered them.

The water was cold and my breath froze, a giant ice block below my heart. I waded beyond him, bobbed there like a balloon. Weightless.

Tara Laskowski's short story collection, *Bystanders*, won the Balcones Fiction Prize and was hailed by Jennifer Egan as "a bold, riveting mash-up of Hitchcockian suspense and campfire-tale chills." She is

Tara Laskowski

also the author of the flash fiction collection *Modern Manners for Your Inner Demons*, tales of dark etiquette. Her fiction has been published in W. W. Norton's *Flash Fiction International, The New Black, Alfred Hitchcock's Mystery Magazine, Mid-American Review,* and other places. Since 2010, she has been the editor of the online flash fiction journal *SmokeLong Quarterly.*

Randall Brown :
What a Beautiful Dream

[From *The Tishman Review*, Vol. 2, Issue 3, 2016]

My aunt had a puppet made to look like her dead daughter, Peach. When I stayed with her that summer, the Peach-puppet sat at the table by the pool with the two of us, my uncle already gone. I'd come as Peach's replacement, even though I was a boy, someone to reanimate my aunt.

"They used to think the sun orbited the earth." My aunt picked at her salad niçoise, separating each ingredient—green beans, olives, lettuce, tuna, potatoes, onions, egg, capers—into its own space. "Did you hear that, Samuel?"

I shook my head no, my mouth full of mixed-up niçoise, the best thing I'd ever eaten. Peach had died in a plane, a family trip to Casa De Campo, an anaphylactic reaction to something in the airline food; they thought pesto. Imagine her drowning in the air, unable to find breath after breath, throat closing, that awful silence.

"I hear laughter." She sipped her whiskey. "I think it's coming from the clouds."

I checked. Not a cloud in sight. Just an airplane, its exhaust an ash-trail against the brilliant blue. It looked like a sea. A sea in the sky. The exhaust now a wake. Peach, the puppet, stared straight ahead like my aunt. Imagine the rest of the plane ride, their dead daughter in her window seat, above clouds, staring into the sun.

Peach had been sometimes quiet, like now, contemplating, awaiting her moment to bust out. I tried to be like her, but my Peach impression did nothing for my aunt. She remained half-present. When she fell asleep in the lounge chair, I ate her niçoise, too. Her personal chef came out to remove the plates, patted my head, and Peach's. Oh, Peach. Sad, silent Peach.

A red curl of Peach's hair dropped in front of her copper eyes. I moved it back in place, stroked her carnation-pink cheek. Her arms—permanently outstretched, palms upward—made me check the sky for rain. She wore a white T-shirt, a black-stitched face over her heart, X's for eyes. Over it, to keep her from getting a chill, her mother had chosen a gray hoodie with purple stripes. I reached behind Peach, wanting to straighten things, felt instead the hole. My arm snaked up her back, went inside, a subterranean cavern, cold and empty. Her head turned to me.

"Pick me up. Go ahead. Remember my voice as we built a tower of cards to the ceiling."

Yes, deep like a frog's. One more, she'd croak, and I—trembling—would hand her the cards, and sometimes she'd drop them before she could place them and they'd flutter-by, flutter-by, never hitting the tower, flutter-by.

"Remember," Peach-puppet said, "when my father came out of the kitchen with a meat thermometer stabbed in his shoulder. 'Do you see,' he said to us, 'what she's done now?' Mother came running to hear me say to Father, 'She must've been very hungry.' The three of us collapsed in laughter. You, too, Samuel! Another time Father had strewn trash all over the kitchen, saying, 'You'll see. Someone will make it disappear.'

You and I swam through the garbage, coast to coast, Mother and Father clapping."

How often I'd dreamed of Peach's house—so much space, so much wild life, so far away from my life in that tiny trailer next to the tent revivals, all those tongues speaking their own languages, like a TV getting all the channels at once with no way to drown them out.

My aunt woke up. "So sly," she said.

"What do you mean?" said Peach in that frog's croak.

"Waiting so long."

Randall Brown is the author of the award-winning flash fiction collection *Mad to Live*. His work appears in *The Rose Metal Press Field Guide to Writing Flash Fiction; The Norton Anthology of Hint Fiction; Funny Bone: Flashing for Comic Relief;* Grey House Publishing's *Critical Insights: American Short Story* and *Critical Insights: Flash Fiction;* and *The Best Small Fictions 2015*. He is also the founder and managing editor of FlashFiction.Net, along with Matter Press and its *Journal of Compressed Creative Arts*. He received his MFA from Vermont College and teaches in Rosemont College's MFA in Creative Writing Program.

Heather McQuillan
Sisters

[From *Flash Frontier: An Adventure in Short Fiction*, December 2016 micro issue]

Elspeth's fingers touch air above the piano. "Can you hear this? I'm playing the notes between the keys."

Our mother swoops in, swipes my sister off the stool, smacks down the lid. Elspeth staggers to stand, clutching at her head where thin skin has split. Blood seeps between her fingers. She smiles.

I put down my book and hand her a tea towel folded into a pad.

Our mother has gone outside to weep and Elspeth has returned to playing nothing. I hear her discordant music at each turn of the page.

Heather McQuillan is a writing teacher, and her novels for young readers have won awards, including the Tom Fitzgibbon Award (2005), and have been recognized as a Storylines Notable Book in

2006 and 2012. In 2016, Heather won the New Zealand National Flash Fiction Day Competition and the Micro Madness Award. Her flash fiction appears regularly on *Flash Frontier* and her poetry is published in a number of anthologies, including *Landfall 231*. She is currently a Masters of Creative Writing student at Massey University and is working toward her first flash fiction collection. She is from New Zealand.

Joy Katz :
Don't Walk

[From *FLASHed: Sudden Stories in Comics & Prose*
(Pressgang, 2016)]

What is it stops traffic? A hand would be a dirty flag, at dusk.
There was no hand. A man tucked his hands into his jacket.

The intensity of an instant spun through dusk. A dusk full
of clutter: haggy treeline; loose teeth of strip mall; the dollar
store sign you might as well toss, it's thin and it's offgassing.
Five p.m. kid-in-the-car hour I haul myself through.

The minute split—December smeared the windshield,
vapor-lit the backseat—*Tell me a story, mama.*

Well, there was this dragon . . .

In the moment of *there was this dragon . . .* , in the hour of
every day, he, in the epoch of *and then, one time*, in the space
between my palm and my glove—the space that is the sole
warmth on Earth—my girl curls her spine against the booster.

She leans back—her expression is bored. Is so trusting as
to be bored. Looks out the window—there is not a drop of fear
in her face—I can't bear it—

In the metal of the hour of trash bin, of summer canned, a
temperate climate somewhere off behind a cupboard door—in
this hour when I do not want anything—isn't this a kind of

freedom—to not want anything?—to be emptied of all but this getting-through, offering a story: *and then, one time*

between walk and don't, between the idea of turning and the first degree of turn, palm in glove on steering wheel, a man stepped so

freely—in front of my car. A man in front of my car—

pure shape—indecipherable cause—*see me,* says this shape. The man is black, gray-jacketed, stepping out, no glance at me, no warning hand, stepping out into (the road suddenly all missing) snow, in front of me—

head down, as if he has made up his mind about something. Where did this story start.

Holding his head as if he has made up his mind about— me, about us? about something. Steps in front of my car with a—certainty, a patience even, that widens a minute—*and then what, mama?*—into an ocean. He steps with

faith? that I—stretch out all the muscles of my legs—in the ocean of instant of ongoingness—oh yes, faith that I will stop the story—a story we are in the middle of, this hour, the getting-through, this street, this block, this city, the all I have, the all we have—*Mama!*—my girl slams back into the booster seat—

Once there was a woman. Once there was a white woman. Once there was a woman in a car. A five-year-old girl in a purple scarf, in the backseat. Once, a black man stepped out into the street into the roar of snow and ice, five o'clock— where did this story start.

His faith I will brake is large as my doubt in everything. I am not certain I will ever be alive in a next minute. This is how I live. A mother. All the time. Snapped. Like a hand off a mannequin. This man steps, pure shape, with a power muffled in snow, a power in the choice he has made, of slowness—just steps out as if—*and then what happens?*—well, he has a power

I have to accord. Even: to admire. Has reversed the power between us, has seized, even, my legs—he is in them—react! *I*

see you. See him. In a too-small jacket, hands tucked in. Gray shape in the gray dusk. Press press press my legs to the floor—
He wants? to die—wants to take me
from my daughter? take us all from—what. Take us to—
See me! and I
in the hour become the bottom of an elevator coming toward me, iron cube sliding so precisely into iron box—it fits precisely because time is precise—
in the hundredth of a second in which I have not hit him, not yet, *and then, one time*—in the next hundredth-second coming toward us—I do want something—to know the end of this story—
I spin toward the bridge, the curb, the hooded walk sign with its crisp white walking man blinking and blinking and blinking—but the story doesn't end here.

Joy Katz writes poetry and nonfiction. Her work in progress, *White: An Abstract*, is an attempt to document American whiteness. Her latest collection of poems, *All You Do Is Perceive*, was a National Poetry Series finalist. Katz is cofounder of and collaborator in the activist art collective Ifyoureallyloveme. The recipient of fellowships from the National Endowment for the Arts, the Heinz Foundation, and the Barbara Deming Fund, Katz teaches in the MFA program at Chatham University and in Carlow University's Madwomen in the Attic workshops. She lives in Pittsburgh, Pennsylvania.

Ian Seed :

Filer à l'anglaise

[From *Identity Papers* (Shearsman, 2016)]

At an Italian bookfair, I met two authors, a man and a woman. They read out to a small audience clustered around one of the stalls. As a foreigner, I felt obliged to show generosity and buy one of their books, but they were expensive, and when I flicked through their pages, I could see how dull and difficult they were. I decided to sneak away without buying anything. A back path took me to a high, steep bank leading up to a busy road. I climbed the bank and almost fell at the top because the edge of the road was crumbling away due to recent floods. Luckily, there was a branch I could grab hold of. However, once on the road, I could see just how dangerous it was, with cars coming at top speed in both directions, and no path for pedestrians. Yet I could not face going back to the fair, for now down below I could see some of the crowd pointing up at me, including the two authors whose books I didn't want.

Ian Seed

Ian Seed's most recent publications are *Italian Lessons* (LikeThis-Press, 2017), *The Thief of Talant* (Wakefileld, 2016; the first translation into English of Pierre Reverdy's 1917 experimental novel, *Le Voleur de Talan*), *Identity Papers* (Shearsman, 2016), and *Makers of Empty Dreams* (Shearsman, 2014). His work often crosses over from prose poetry to short fiction and back again and has been featured on BBC Radio 3's "The Verb," and appears in *The Best British Poetry 2014* and *The Forward Book of Poetry 2017*. He has a PhD in European Languages and Cultures, and now lectures in creative writing at the University of Chester in the UK.

Carrie Cooperider :
Stutterers

[From *Friday Flash Fiction*, November 21, 2016]

People wouldn't quit cutting ahead of me in the line for sleep so I gave up, turning my back on the smug curvature of earth spooned into the night. A lunar-shaped cusp had tracked its cramped orbit around my wrist by the time my watch crash-landed on your bedside table. You had struggled for words, slapping your thigh to spur your panicked tongue to form the requisite sounds. You managed "I," and could have done "you," but I knew you'd never get the "L" word in between, so I said it for both of us: "I luh-luh-luh- lie to you, too."

Carrie Cooperider's writing has been published in *Cabinet, Antioch Review, The Southampton Review, Artishock, NY Tyrant, Autre,* and elsewhere. Cooperider has an MFA in visual art from Queens College, New York, attended the Whitney Independent Studio Program, and is currently an MFA candidate in the low-residency writing program at Bennington College, in Vermont. She lives in New York City.

Anne Valente :
A Personal History of Arson

[From *Puerto del Sol*, Issue 51.2, Spring 2016]

Picture frames. Photo albums. Family portraits, snapshots, matte prints.

Known melting points: aluminum, 1220 degrees Fahrenheit.

Polystyrene: 266 degrees. Copper: 1083 degrees.

Beware assuming gas burners as cause. Even every burner activated full blast leaves no room for combustion due to drafts, due to cracks in windows and between floorboards and among bricks and the gaps of screened windows, keeping gas below the danger of a flash point, all of which leak air from a home, imperceptibly, all of the time.

Dishes. Wedding china. Flatware. Antique silver, ladles, cutting boards, spoons.

Steel: 1400. Ethyl alcohol: 1540. Gasoline: 1490. Stove propane: 1778.

Magnets collected from family travels: Nashville. Yellowstone. Bar Harbor, Maine. Sarasota, Myrtle Beach, the Wisconsin Dells, the Grand Canyon.

Calcium, bone: 1547.

Human skin: just 162 degrees between flame and disintegration.

Beware the kitchen. Beware oil. Vegetable, animal, fish, linseed, corn, olive, sunflower: every oil except mineral, the potential to ignite spontaneously.

Boxed cereal, dried pasta, crackers. Canned tomatoes and beans and beets. A spice rack of cinnamon, curry powder, turmeric, paprika. A refrigerator impervious to burning, left standing and full of half-spoiled milk, plain yogurt, hardened cheese, a half-dozen mottled eggs. Wilting lettuce, jars of mayonnaise and mustard and pickles, apples and potatoes and pears still intact, their solid roundness untouched by flame.

Beware open windows, the drafts of which offer false points of origin. Beware wind, the pulling of air, large areas of damage made to look like a source.

Drapes, curtains, window blinds, doorknobs. Light fixtures and light bulbs, a cracking hiss as their glass heats and explodes. Ironing board. So many clothes. Stockings, leggings, wool socks, corduroy pants and jeans and sweatpants, collared shirts and a cacophony of tees gathered from sporting events, thrift stores, marathons, vacations. Knit hats and mittens and gloves, scarves and earmuffs and swimsuits and beach towels.

Beware charcoals. Hickory. Oak. Ash. All impulsively sparked to flame. Coffee tables. Couches. Inherited side tables and buffets, passed down from grandparents and great-grandparents. Bookcases full of children's books, reference books, classics of literature, a single baby book.

Carbon dioxide at six percent: headache, dizziness, drowsiness.

Carbon dioxide at 10 percent: a lack of breathing.

Carbon dioxide: heavier than air. Forms pockets of lethal concentration.

Beware a history: folded notes, movie ticket stubs, bottle caps, blown-out birthday candles, school photos. Diaries with tiny keys, journals of drawings, sketches of teachers and peers and turning maples beyond the classroom window. A miniature box of porcelain kittens, tiny owls, small frogs, a minuscule gumball machine. A jewelry box: emerald earrings. Collected necklaces. Textbooks wrapped in brown grocery bags. A bag of gemstones. Fool's gold. Glow-in-the-dark stars stuck to a charred ceiling.

Beware investigation: mine for mental state. Determine cause and origin. Secure medical records. Obtain fire reports from chief officers, establish condition of found building. Inspect for bruises, broken bones. Make maps, diagrams, sketches. Note a pugilistic position. Note a charring of skin, or else not: split skin. Bone fractures emanating outward. Loss of tissue. Steam blisters. Soot in mouth, nostrils. Indication of carbon dioxide in the bloodstream, lividity in colored patches as blood settles. Note particular damage to the head, indication of malicious intent. Note visible bite marks, claw marks, stab wounds, bullet wounds, defense wounds, cuts.

Wrap in cloth sheets. Preserve the clothing.

Remove dentures, bridgework, false teeth. Canvass for witnesses.

Surround what remains. Take photographs.

Preserve all artifacts, everything saved.

Beware shattered porcelain. Coffee mugs. Broken pieces of Mickey Mouse's ears brought home from Disney World driving through the night from Florida to the Midwest, the highway's center line a mirrored flash to the sky's stars. Plastic flatware. Melted in cupboards. Cups and wine glasses without stems and burst bottles of pinot noir. Puffed coats. Missouri winter. A black leather jacket stuffed in the back of the closet. Love letters. Notes saved from junior high, from anniversaries, birthdays, Valentine's Day. Bubbled handwriting dotted with hearts. The salt taste of sweat. Threads of hair still clinging to a mattress, afternoon light slanting through windows and kaleidoscoping the walls.

Baby book of inked footprints, smudged palm prints. Small as ducklings, thimbles. Beginnings. *The Cat in the Hat. Goodnight Moon.* This book belongs to. Soccer ball. Jersey Knit shorts and Dri-Fit shirts and the spikes of cleats clotted with grass. Mix tape. Videotape. Board games. Monopoly. Candyland. Hungry Hungry Hippos. Barrel of Monkeys. Lincoln Logs. Tarot cards and playing cards and a Ouija board used only once, a sixth-grade sleepover when the planchette moved and so many hands flinched away.

Anne Valente is the author of the novel *Our Hearts Will Burn Us Down* (William Morrow/HarperCollins, 2016), and the short story collection *By Light We Knew Our Names* (Dzanc Books, 2014). Her second novel, *Utah*, is forthcoming from William Morrow in 2019. Her fiction appears in *One Story, The Kenyon Review, The Southern Review,* and *Ninth Letter* and won a 2015 *Chicago Tribune* Nelson Algren Award. Her essays appear in *The Believer, The Rumpus, Prairie Schooner,* and *The Washington Post.* Originally from St. Louis, Missouri, she currently teaches creative writing at Santa Fe University of Art and Design.

Jen Knox :
Lottery Days

[From *Literary Orphans*, Issue 26: Shirley, 2016]

You told me not to play with matches that summer, so I palmed a corner-store lighter instead. The flame reached for the tip of your blue crayon, until you knocked the lighter from my hands. You wanted to color the sky, you said, and I wouldn't ruin your chance.

I plodded behind, watching socks fall down the backs of your ankles. You explained that this is why we shouldn't buy socks at Odd Lots, which was sometimes Big Lots, because kids knew. Feet knew. The store carried three coat styles, and mine was one. I liked the color for fall, a warm maroon. You tugged at the longer sleeve.

We were both coupled by winter, our hearts twisted like tree trunks. We ate cold shrimp in the living room of a one-bedroom apartment near downtown, watching Power Puff Girls and retelling jokes, adjusting bra straps and headbands, discussing jobs that allowed money of our own. We quantified everything those lottery days, green grapes or tiramisu.

We were plump like prunes that spring, tired of snow. Grown. Perhaps this is why I chose to move somewhere warm. Heart still twisted, I navigated a state that you stitched atop a heart on a pillow that I hugged like a tiny person. I told you

I had a black thumb, a fun term for not understanding the relentlessness of a southern sun. You said talking to plants gives them life, not because they hear you but because they feed on your breath. It doesn't matter why a thing works, so long as it does.

I never told you that I kept the garden for you, a swell of life that you will never see. We never admitted such sentimental things. But it's here now, your garden. It thrives for you beneath a sometimes blue sky.

Jen Knox is a writing coach and community engagement director. Her fiction can be found in *The Adirondack Review*, *Chicago Tribune's Printers Row*, *Chicago Quarterly Review*, *Crannóg*, *Gargoyle*, *The Istanbul Review*, *Modern Shorts* (Fiction Attic Press), *Room Magazine*, *The Santa Fe Writers Project Quarterly*, and *The Saturday Evening Post*. Her collection of stories, *After the Gazebo* (Rain Mountain Press), was nominated for the 2015 Pen/Faulkner, and she earned finalist status in the University of Louisville's Calvino Prize in 2016. Jen's newest collection of fabulist fiction, *The Glass City* (Hollywood Books International, 2017), won the Prize Americana for Prose.

William Woolfitt

Hatchlings

[From *r.kv.r.y quarterly*, vol. xiii. no. 2, 2016]

I join the community patrol to prove my brothers wrong, my brothers who say I am too moony to find the nests, too scared of *hueveros* to walk the beach at night. The patrol sends us out in pairs. We walk the black sand beach, we bring grease pens and plastic shopping bags, we search for leatherback turtles come ashore to lay eggs. My brothers are older, taller, with muscles that they flex and eyes like cacao seeds. My cousin is older than my brothers, he has long crinkly hair, he plays marimba, and it's better if I am paired with him. With oldest brother, I walk the kilometers of moonless beach. Middle brother and I try to hear a leatherback rasp and snort, over the noise of the waves, panting as she scoops out the pit-nest where she lays her clutch of eggs. Cousin and I look for flipper tracks, the ever-so-slightly darker sand where a leatherback may have dragged herself. My brothers act like they see me with new eyes, forget to call me girl-lips and *niñita*. I know it will not last. I am the youngest, the clumsy one, the weak swimmer. My brothers love to joke and tease and change the rules. Two weeks after I join, oldest brother pins me down and fills my shorts with wet sand.

Unless we get there first, *hueveros* slip out from the tall grass, steal the eggs and sell them as black market aphrodisiacs to disco owners, to sad men hoping to get a charge from a glass of slime. My brothers despise the slime drinkers, say that a real man does not drink eggs, that *hueveros* are cowards, that I may need to try the eggs, or else I will always be a baby rat, pale and hairless and shrill when I speak. Cousin says that *hueveros* do the work of their fathers and grandfathers, some are not scoundrels, he knows one with too many children to feed.

I repeat the novena of Our Lord, I ask for eyes to find and ears to catch. At first, all I wanted was to impress my cousin and brothers, but now I want to help the turtles, too. I make prayers to Virgen del Carmen, I inspect the sand, the water and sky, everything dark, even the surf-foam and the clouds, dark as burnt wood, dark as Virgen's beads and wig. And then I spy a pale-spotted carapace, and I drop to my knees. Middle brother congratulates me, says that I am good at tracking, claps me on the back, then he pushes me down, holds my face in the nest so that the eggs drop from the mother, slide down my cheek. Middle brother says, *stick your hand in there.* While her hind-flippers plow the sand back in, I remove from the pit-nest what feels like seventy jellied ping-pong balls and place them inside the bag that my brother holds open. Seventy times, I hold a turtle egg in my hand, each of them fragile and squishy and warm.

In pairs, we carry eggs to the manmade nests of the town *criadera.* We bury them there, we keep watch, night and day. Oldest brother dribbles a *fútbol*, asks me to help him with his drills, gives up when he sees how awkward I am. Middle brother strikes matches, smokes *cigarillos*. He asks me if I want to smoke; I refuse; he rolls his eyes. Cousin carves a mallet, teaches me card tricks. Again and again, I dig a hole in the sand, I put my hand in the hole and cover it, then I wiggle my fingers and spring my hand free. *It might be like this*, I tell myself. My hand like a baby turtle, newly hatched and digging out. We chase away crabs and stray dogs, we watch for *hueveros* eager to come creeping with wire-cutters and spades. We pinch ourselves awake and eat Pringle chips and flatten the cans.

The hatchlings break through their shells with carunkle-teeth and tunnel up through sand. We carry them to the lip of the tide, we are quiet and careful as altar boys. Craning their tiny necks, the *tortugitos* search for light, gaps in the clouds, any glimmer or beam. I lift my head, too. I seek the newest pieces of sky, then I watch the *tortugitos* clamber toward the low waves that ease them from the sand.

I keep watch in the *criadera* again, this time with middle brother. Cousin has gone to Siquirres to woo the daughter of a pineapple farmer; older brother drank too much *chicha* and is sick at home. I squat, scoop out a hole, cover my hand, but then I can't get free. Middle brother stands over my hand, grinds with his heel, and I feel grains of sand cutting into me. *The real test isn't getting out of the sand,* he says. *It's the ocean. You know that sharks finish off most of them. And they eat plastic trash, it kills them but they love plastic. I can throw you in the water since you like to pretend.* While he pins my hand with his foot, I feel the cold water he would banish me to, patches of light and dark in the sky that I don't know how to read, and then the lash of waves that would take me down, the burn of salt in my nose, and the spray that chills my skin.

William Woolfitt

What the Beech Tree Knows

[From *Tahoma Literary Review*, Issue 8, 2016]

All that the track-men tip from dumpcarts—rootlets, and clods of dirt, and knuckles of shale—hills up in the July sun. I look out at the tracks while I stand near a beech tree that I know. When I put my hand on its bark, the beech does not quicken or groan. I try to hear its rush of sap, I hold my ear to the trunk, and although I hear nothing, I keep my ear there. At last, I hear a low drumming. But it's only the throb of my blood where my head presses the bark, and even that fades when the track-men call out a work-song: *on the Red Sea shore, Moses smote the water with a two-by-four.*

Too hot to fight the witch-grass and Spanish needles that choke the corn. Flinging my hoe into high thistles, I run into the woods. My aunt will peel a switch; my uncle will vow a beating and track me. I search for rocky overhangs, for earth-folds. For pockets that conceal me like a button, or a soldier's bone dice, or a curl of hair. I tuck myself into dens, boy-sized wallows in the laurel-hells.

My memories of my parents diminish, are nearly gone from the house where we lived, emptied of their personal goods and bric-a-brac, swept and polished and soaped with lye. I get more of them when I go among the trees they knew, glimpses of my mother gathering leaves and pressing them in her shabby Bible, my father showing me how to make bark rubbings, my mother introducing me to trees almost like they were people. When she sang ballads, she sometimes took out the dukes and the ladies, put in walnuts and birches and willows with their long green tresses. From my parents, I know that hickory is for fires that burn longest. And catalpa tree for bait, my father used the worms that ate the catalpa's seedpods when he fished Shavers Fork. Elderberry for the dye my mother called *Queen Esther purple.* Sourwood for the whistles and spoons that I carve, that my uncle sells in Marlinton. And woodpeckered beech for watching black crewmen and horse-teams, the tracks at the edge of my father's land. Branch-sprawled, leaf-shaded, I study the ragged stumps that the track-men leave, and the new bed they smooth, the earth meek and ruled.

Sundays only there is mirth in the house. My uncle and aunt invite the preacher, the elders and their wives, rowdy sons who grapple in the yard. The preacher flashes his big teeth, bangs hymns from my mother's piano that is silent the rest of the week. Between hymns, the preacher takes out his hanky and mops sweat from his forehead, from my mother's ivory keys. When I turn from the piano, I hear an elder say, *he's getting tall.* Another says, *soon he won't be so delicate.* My uncle says, *might work better if there was muscle on his bones.* They talk as if I am not there. If they notice me slipping out the door, they give no sign.

Sometimes, I believe that the beech welcomes me, can be companionable, a holder of secrets. That it may greet me with a shiver that I am sure to miss unless I look carefully. Always, the beech offers me a hiding room. And sawtoothed leaves that cool blisters. And branches that I climb to, and spread flat on until I fade from view, as if I am suited in leaves and the smooth gray bark.

For my mother buried under the walnut, my aunt set out a headstone. For my father's tears, his nights of sleeping on her grave, my uncle locked him in the smokehouse. When my father got loose, he roamed the woods in a breechcloth. He said that his Shawnee grandfather visited his dreams, he was going to make a basket from ash splints that could take him to the stars. My uncle sent my father to the Weston asylum. *When he gets cured*, my aunt said, *he'll come back and thank us. We're improving his property, his boy.* My uncle claimed my father's acres and house. Now he haggles with Deer Creek Lumber Company, sells my father's stands of hemlock, spruce, and white oak. My aunt holds a string to me and takes my measure, makes clothes for me, and cuts my hair, and busies my idle hands.

Best is the cavity of the beech. There is room for my thoughts here, and old voices, the littlest pieces. My father told me, *let the trees show you things.* They sent him away the next day. He told me to do the same with a bee gum I was about to rob, a rabbit before shooting it: *go soft, go slow.* The beech's hollow space is the shape of me if I tuck one arm like a wing, if I stretch the other overhead.

William Woolfitt is the author of three poetry collections: *Beauty Strip* (2014), *Charles of the Desert* (2016), and the forthcoming *Spring Up*

William Woolfitt

Everlasting (Paraclete Press, 2018). His fiction chapbook *The Boy with Fire in His Mouth* (2014) won the Epiphany Editions contest judged by Darin Strauss. His poems and short stories have appeared in *Blackbird, Image, Tin House, The Threepenny Review, Michigan Quarterly Review, The Missouri Review, Epoch, Spiritus,* and other journals. He is the recipient of the Howard Nemerov Scholarship from the Sewanee Writers' Conference and the Denny C. Plattner Award from *Appalachian Heritage.*

Harriot West :
Picking Sunflowers for Van Gogh

[From *KYSO Flash*, Issue 6, Fall 2016]

An Ekphrastic Haibun Story

It's not an easy task. For all his impasto and rough ways with the brush, he's extraordinarily fussy about his flowers. And he hates it when they droop. Sometimes I see him gently cup a sagging bloom. So tenderly it's easy to imagine him helping an old woman lug her pannier up a rickety flight of stairs. I like him then. Despite how demanding he is to work for. Never a word of thanks. My hands stained with pollen, to say nothing of dust rags that look as though they've been steeped in saffron.

It's a pity he isn't fonder of roses. Except for those thorns. Lavender perhaps? I'd fancy that. Brushing my fingertips along

Harriot West

the stalks, carrying their scent throughout the day, dreaming about a wild man with ginger hair and reckless ways.

heat wave
the honey bee's
restless thrum

Harriot West lives in Eugene, Oregon. Her first collection of haibun, *Into the Light* (Mountains and Rivers Press, 2014), tied for first place in the 2015 Haiku Society of America's Mildred Kanterman Book Awards. Her work appears in many journals and anthologies, including *Modern Haiku, KYSO Flash, Haibun Today, Frogpond, Contemporary Haibun Online*, and *The Norton Anthology of Haiku in English*. Honors include Modern Haiku's Best of Issue award for haibun and the Museum of Haiku Literature Award. She is currently at work on her second book of haibun, *Shades of Absence*.

Karen Brennan

10 Birds

[From *Monsters* (Four Way Books, 2016)]

1

When I woke up, birds were entering the room, their voices fluty & sharp-witted. The pillow's fine creases had imprinted themselves on the skin of my cheek. I checked myself for the feeling of dread. This is like taking a temperature and involves a body scan but no instrument. As usual, I remind myself of the bed's great comfort due to expensive memory foam purchased to disguise lumps. Soon everything in the world will duplicate, memory foam as hat.

2

I was struck by the presence of birds tiptoeing across the floor boards. I actually despised this pillow, the way it rebounded from my head's weight seemed to herald the dread I felt. As if we have power to affect nothing. I scanned the room—a little light scurried up the walls. The man beside me was dead to the world. If I had to duplicate myself I wouldn't know where to begin.

3

The man beside me rolled over as was his custom as if he were telling me to go back to sleep. Too many birds in the room, now they were beside me flicking their feathers. I never cared for their song, which was unmelodic but let's face it, birds were a metaphor for the dread I felt. I scanned the back of my hand for some kind of indication that time would heal all wounds. My pillow slipped to the floor and with it one of the smallest birds upon whose face I read an expression of weariness.

4

At this point, I believed things had changed places with other things. In place of the man beside me was his pillow. This was curious because I knew the pillow was a metaphor for weari-ness & the birds seemed to be hiding. I wondered about the light, its creases within other creases felt like one more dupli-cation, like a memory unmoored to its moment, a phrase that occurred to me as I regarded the man beside me.

5

Sunlight seeped through the wooden blinds & I heard the birds rattling around in the trees. I heard the two-tone note of the mourning dove, a sound residing in my memory & ushering in a cluster of images from that era—brown dust of backyard, the apricot tree which someone cut down. How the birds loved those apricots. There was another man beside me. The walls mint green, not a good choice.

6

Dread was ushering in my body, dead to the world, as if on all four corners the birds were bearing with me. Where had I been that such melodies prevailed? There'd been a time, I felt certain, that duplicated this time, but was not remembered. The two-tone notes of the cluster of mourning doves were as ghosts, some shadowy particle of half-tone objects that flew by too fast. I tried to awaken the man beside me but in his place the creases on the pillow were transferring themselves to the air, whipped up by birds' constant feather flicking. How comfortable was the bed with its memory foam, as memory is always a comfort, ushering in feelings of a life well connected & aptly metaphorized by a series of floating objects.

7

As though I had never slept at all, so stationary were the room's accouterments. The man beside me let out a groan & I knew for certain that this time was an exact duplication of another time, a time in which I'd been sleeping beside another man in a room whose walls were mint green. For a moment, then, I felt dread creeping along the pillow & imprinting itself on my cheek. I was aware of a hallucination of birds but these were symptoms, not exactly metaphors, since they existed outside the window in chorus.

8

I woke to sleeping on my hand instead of the pillow & what I'd thought were the pillow creases imprinted on my cheek was actually a map of my future, complete with luck lines & love pits. The man beside me seemed to have vanished but the memory foam held his shape like a saucer holds a cup out of which a cluster of objects might suddenly spring & proceed to float across the room. I was thirsty. The two-tone note of my dream accompanied the light which scurried up the walls which were not mint green but interrupted by the slatted blinds through which sunlight seeped. I perceived a little cornice of dread in my body scan but I dismissed it as a shadowy column bearing the weight of memory (foam).

9

It was green & frightening. Who was I kidding, the birds had arrived & they were insistent. Although there was no instrument involved, the scan of my body proceeded as mournfully as the little two-toned notes of the mourning doves. I was searching for the man beside me, eyes closed against light, but encountered only the memory foam, the place where he'd been before he rolled over. Such melodies prevailed in a manner that came closer to a cluster of floating objects flicking against the scurried light on the walls. The birds were metaphors for ghosts & I removed my hand from beneath the creased pillow.

10

It was in this particular room & bed, in no particular order. If the man had been a bird, his voice sharp-witted, fluty instead of dead to the world. My feeling of dread so familiar it is an old friend like the light which exists in & out of creases whose creases are two-noted & definite as opposed to the shadow play of objects I made up for this occasion. The man may or may not be beautiful, the mint green walls of my past should not be inflicted on anyone & the birds have fled. In another less metaphorical sense everything duplicates & reduplicates which makes memory foam redundant & antithetical to waking, either beside or not beside a person who has rolled away or who has moved a pillow to replicate what may occur to him, unmoored to the moment, remote & indispensable.

Karen Brennan is the author of seven books of varying genres, including three poetry collections, three books of fiction (including *Monsters*), and a memoir. An AWP Award winner in short fiction (*Wild Desire*, 1990) and a recipient of a National Endowment of the Arts fellowship, Brennan's poetry, fiction, and nonfiction have appeared in anthologies from Graywolf, Norton, Penguin, Spuytin Duyvil, Georgia Press, and the University of Michigan Press, among others. She is Professor Emerita at the University of Utah and teaches at the Warren Wilson MFA Program for Writers.

Matt Sailor :
Sea Air

[From *Five Points*, Vol. 17, No. 3, Fall 2016]

Dad was on furlough that whole summer, so the only vacation we could afford was the beach.

Mom seemed concerned—was it safe? But it had been a hard year and I could see it in her eyes. She needed a break.

"You don't want to go there," said Mickey, a boy in my algebra class who used to pull my hair at recess. "There's still people underneath. At night they walk the coast." His family was headed to the mountains like everyone else, to ski on synthetic snow.

We stayed at a Radisson that had been in the distant suburbs before the rise. It wasn't safe to swim—high Atlantic winds were sending debris in on the tides. So we stood on the balcony, watching the surf crash and break against the foundations of demolished houses. On clear days you could see the tops of drowned buildings on the horizon, where the city had been.

Our last night, I took Dad's bird-watching binoculars out on the balcony. I couldn't sleep. I couldn't stop thinking of rooms full of water, bodies trapped inside, bloated and blue.

Out in the surf, wading knee deep in the water, I saw a man. Soaking wet, pacing back and forth, his hands dead at his sides. I couldn't make out his face. But I was sure. I opened the door to Mom and Dad's adjoining room. Mom slept quietly, alone. Where Dad had been, nothing. A tangle of disturbed sheets.

Matt Sailor lives in Portland, Oregon. His fiction and essays have appeared in publications such as *AGNI, Barrelhouse, Day One,* and *Hobart.* His awards include a Paul Bowles Fellowship from Georgia State University, inclusion in *Wigleaf*'s Top 50 (Very) Short Fictions, and a 2014 National Endowment for the Arts fellowship in fiction. He holds an MFA from Georgia State University, and has previously served as editor-in-chief of *New South*, fiction editor of *The Mondegreen*, and an associate editor of *NANO Fiction*.

Eugenie Montague :
Breakfast

[From *Tin House* ("Flash Fridays"), 2016]

There are thick pieces of toast, but his mother is absent, even though she did place the plate in front of him and now leans against the counter watching him eat. In fact, she is waiting for him to ask for something: more butter, another flavor of jam, cinnamon, a different knife—one without these small flecks of orange corroding the teeth. She had not noticed these spots when she set the table, but she can see them clearly now, very clearly. Everything blurs but that burnt orange rust on ridged stainless steel.

He does not ask for another knife. He picks up the knife he has been given and slices through the butter, which is pale yellow and more liquid than solid, because the butter lives in a glass container on the kitchen counter, and the fall has been unseasonably warm, and the kitchen has many windows. The jam—strawberry, more solid than the butter—spreads easily across the toast, except for three thick lumps of strawberry, preserved almost in their entirety. These will not spread and when he looks at them on his toast, he imagines biting into them, something tough, then a soft bursting between his teeth, and he knows he wants to avoid this feeling. She watches the edge of the knife scrape these chunks of strawberry onto his plate, where they lay mushy, small chewed-up tongues, seeds like engorged taste buds. Inside her, the nausea rises quickly; she feels bile, hot and abrading, burst into her throat. He sees her smile, but she is looking through him to a spot in the future when he has left for school and she can lie down again.

At school, he has started to fall asleep during story hour and, when his teacher, Mrs. Dorothy, lets him, he stays curled up on his mat through the art period that follows, not waking when the other children rise and put their mats away, line up by the door and stomp loudly down the bricked hallway. Mrs. Dorothy has begun to meet him at his bus, where she leads him to the school cafeteria and feeds him spoonfuls of peanut butter from an industrial-sized tub, or cores an apple, placing slice after slice in his warm, pink hand. When the bell rings, she shuffles them both, late, to the classroom where the other children see him enter the room with his teacher. He feels special for the extra attention, but when he told his mother, she cried and went to take a bath and listen to music, loudly. When he went to find her, she was lying in cold water, and the music had stopped. Now, when she says Mrs. Dorothy's name, she says it with an edge to it, like a knife, he thinks, slicing through the soft butter of Mrs. Dorothy's flesh, which rolls at her stomach and plumps up at the top of her dress; he has put his head there and listened to her tell a story. He does not sit on his mother's lap when she tells a story, but sometimes he lies under the covers with her while she reads to him from long, sad books about animals that never stay safe.

And so, for the past two weeks, she has gotten up with him in the morning, placed two pieces of toast in front of him, and watched him eat, ready always to hand him a different condiment or melt a piece of cheddar cheese on top, or to serve him a different breakfast altogether: shredded wheat with three spoonfuls of sugar, bacon heated in the microwave on a piece of paper towel, French toast—bread saturated in a bright eggy mixture, pliable and weak and threatening to fall apart as she transfers each piece to the stove. Granola, scrambled eggs, waffles, oatmeal, pancakes, eggs in a hole, donuts, sour white yogurt with pools of water on top, blueberry muffins, which seem to her bruised and rotting even when they are freshly baked. Anything, she would make him anything, to ensure he leaves her house full.

Eugenie Montague earned her MFA from the University of California, Irvine. Her short fiction has been published by National Public Radio, Amazon, *Faultline, Mid-American Review, Fiction Southeast,* and "Flash Fridays," a flash fiction series from *Tin House* and the Guardian Books Network. Her hybrid work *Treating Attachment Disorder* was the winner of the 2016 Eggtooth Editions' chapbook contest. She lives in El Paso, Texas, where she is working on her first novel.

Christopher DeWan :
The Atheist of Dekalb Street

[From *HOOPTY TIME MACHINES: fairy tales for grown ups* (Atticus Books, 2016)]

In our town, the Irish go to Irish church, the Italians go to Italian church, the Polish go to Polish church, no one knows any Protestants, and the only time we see each other is when one of the churches throws a weekend carnival and shuts down the street for days.

So we were confused already by the atheist lady who lived on Dekalb Street, and even more so when she started to bear stigmata on her hands and feet. They started gently, like bruises, but they entrenched, and when she could no longer get around easily because of them, my dad told me I should go to her house and offer to help, because it was the right thing to do, even though she was atheist and unbaptized.

"What happens to her when she dies?" I asked my dad.

"I don't know," he answered.

I rode my bike up Dekalb Street and knocked on her door. "Hey, lady, do you need any help?"

I saw her through the screen door, sitting at her kitchen table with her feet in a basin of water. She was wearing a blue dress with flowers and black-rimmed glasses. I'd never really seen her before.

"What can you do?" she asked.

"I can do wheelies on my bike and catch frogs and make good sound effects with my mouth."

"What kind of sound effects?"

I showed her my best water-drop sound, which I make by tapping my finger to my cheek while making a sort of fish face. "I can do a better water drop than that," she said, and she puckered up her face and flicked her own cheek, and her water-drop sound was pretty good.

"Is it true you have the stigmata?" I asked her.

She held out her hands and turned them over so I could see the bloody spots on both sides.

"Is it because you're a sinner?"

She pulled her hands away. "Who told you I was a sinner?"

"No one."

"Good, because I'm not. Maybe I'm a saint." She pulled her feet out of the basin of bloody water. "I don't need any help from you today. Come back tomorrow."

The next day, I went back to the woman's house on Dekalb Street. This time, I brought a vial of Holy Water that my mom kept in her night table.

"Why do you think that'll help me?" she asked when I offered it to her.

"Do you want to try it?"

She shrugged and held out her hands and I sprinkled the Holy Water over them. It seeped into the holes in her hands and dripped straight through.

"Any better?" I asked.

She shook her head.

"This is the Irish kind of Holy Water. Maybe you need the Polish kind or the Italian kind."

"Maybe," she said.

"Do atheists have Holy Water?"

She limped over to her liquor cabinet and pulled out an amber bottle. "Everyone has Holy Water," she said, and poured herself a drink.

Over the next days, the stigmata got worse, so the woman couldn't even walk, and I decided to spend more time at her house, taking out trash and mowing her lawn. She had a bookshelf full of stories she let me read while she rested on the sofa.

Other people started coming, too: people from the Irish newspaper and the Italian newspaper and the Polish newspaper. People with casseroles of Irish food and Italian food and Polish food. Priests came to her door, but she chased them away, and a doctor came, but she chased him away, too.

"Don't you want to get better?" I asked her.

"He's just a priest from another religion," she said.

While she slept, I wiped her hands and feet until the rags were filled with blood, and she'd wake seeming to feel better. "You're a good boy," she said, but she was an atheist, so I didn't know if she knew what she was talking about.

"How come you don't have a husband?" I asked her once.

"How come you don't have any manners?" she answered.

By now, a crown of scabs had broken out on her forehead, and she spent all her days sleeping, in a fever state. "Are you scared you're going to die?" I asked.

"Why should I be scared?"

But I could tell from her eyes that she was scared.

I went to the bathroom and filled a basin with water, all the way to the top, and carried it back to where she was lying, careful not to spill it. "You need to sit up now," I told her. "This is important." She used her weak arms to pull herself to sitting, and then I poured the basin of water over her head, all of it, so it soaked her nightgown transparent, so it made her hair into thick brown icicles and ran a river between her breasts and puddled a reservoir between her legs, and brought out the smell of her, the smell of a woman who had spent too many weeks lying on a couch in strange fear and unexplained blood, and I told her, "I baptize you in the name of the Father, the Son, and the Holy Ghost, amen," and it's okay, it was water from the sink, the atheist kind, but it's okay, I understand now, that's what Holy Water is, the believing part.

Christopher DeWan is author of *HOOPTY TIME MACHINES: fairy tales for grown ups*, a collection of domestic fabulism. He has published more than fifty stories in journals including *Bodega, Gravel, Hobart, Passages North,* and *Wigleaf,* and has been nominated twice for the Pushcart Prize. As a screenwriter, he has had television projects with The Chernin Group and Indomitable Entertainment, has collaborated on properties for Bad Robot, Paramount, Universal, and the Walt Disney Company, and is recipient of a fellowship from the International Screenwriters' Association. He currently teaches at the University of California, Riverside, and lives in Los Angeles.

Na'amen Gobert Tilahun :
Culture House

[From *Eleven Eleven*, Issue 21, 2016]

This new home is the same as the last—loyal to colors I remember from my youth. It's been a long time since these shades of green and gold were my whole world, now they merely shield cold concrete and metal. It is hard to remember when the view outside my house was rolling amber hills. Is history always this distant and faded for those who are erased?

I nod at the men who pass, barely able to make out their faces through the frosted glass helmets. Slowly, unsteady in their suits—layers between us and any touch that might infect or comfort—they lumber out of my house. The cupboards are stocked with enough for weeks and there will be a food drop at the airlock long before I run out. I close my eyes and hope I'll be here longer than the last house, that here I will find safety if not a home.

No never a home, never again. All that is left is hope that the gawkers and the photographers will finally allow me to try to forget.

While cooking my lunch I sing a simple prayer-song, learned at my mother's feet, taught to my children and grandchildren as they knelt at mine. Not that it matters now, they are all gone from me. I no longer sing from belief but to wash the taste of bitter herbs from my mouth that always accompanies these memories. However, my voice does nothing to sooth the constant silence.

The subsidized computer they provided lays open, blinking with messages from family and friends. I ignore it and take my plate of food out to the porch. I don't like all this electronic communication. I miss the rough weight of paper in my hands, feeling all of the writer's emotion pressed into physical marks on the page. So many things I've already lost and now I cannot even have that. And in any case it is not the same as being among my family, no matter how many videos we exchange.

"No real way to tell if the virus can pass through paper" is what they say. Their words have damaged my world too much to believe them even when passed through so many filters.

Halfway through my meal a car pulls up, not the shiny, black sedans I'm used to, but an old, ratty Jeep that screams paparazzi. The woman who gets out is short and squat, her pale white skin already turning red in the bright sun.

I know what I am meant to do. Go inside, call the numbers by my phone, report this and wait for them to come. They'll come, take her away, and hours from now I will again be sitting in a trailer dragged behind cars containing heavily suited men on my way to a new house. Identical to this one.

All this to save something years dead.

I hate these people, the men and women who came to us wearing the self-delusion of savior and invariably say they did not know their language would be a virus to us. They did not know how it would latch onto my people's voices and warp our history into the past and our future to nothing.

How quickly the sounds of my childhood faded. Wiped so clean that I am the last who remembers the lilts and accents that once made us a people. I am another remnant for their museums, another thing lost to their progress.

Would it be so bad?

I am tired.

Of everything.

All the time.

Perhaps I am meant to be infected, to let my language slip away. It would be an easy thing, to hack this prison and walk out of confinement. I will kiss this woman, hold her body against mine, let the virus take me with the touch I've so long been denied.

I could be with them, again the center of my family, my five children moving from room to room, grandchildren underfoot as they speak and sing and tell stories.

Except.

The stories will not be the same, in the conqueror's tongue. None of the words, none of the sounds, none of the history will be the same. Our concepts, our culture that molded the story is lost forever in the translation

This culture which now numbers me.

The choice should be harder but my life has been nothing but hard choices, mostly made by others in recent memory. My culture is history and language, colors and songs true but it is also family, growth and change not the static frozen life I sit in.

Swallowing the last bite on my food, I smile as it warms my belly. I look back at the house and the messages waiting for me, then back to the woman. She fiddles with the airlock, the camera dangling from one elbow, charged and flashing.

I set the plate down and make my decision.

Na'amen Gobert Tilahun holds a BA from San Francisco State University and an MFA from Mills College. He writes in multiple genres and has had work appear in *Fantasy Magazine*, io9.com, *Queers Dig Time Lords*, *Faggot Dinosaur*, *Full of Crows*, *The Big Click*, *Eleven Eleven*, *Spelling the Hours*, *Loose Lips*, and more. Named one of 13 Bay Area Writers to Watch/Read in 2016 by 7x7 magazine, his debut novel, *The Root*, was named an ALA Rainbow List Top Ten book for 2017. The sequel novel, *The Tree*, will be released in 2017.

Scott Garson : **Writer**

[From *Fanzine* (24.02.16)]

On TV once, late at night, when I was a kid, in my teens, I saw a guy who was homeless.

Maybe he was homeless.

He looked like Jesus. I remember him like that.

Like wearing a cloth diaper. Though Jesus didn't wear a diaper, I'm aware.

The guy kept appearing. This was a documentary. Something of that kind. And he kept showing up. Things were a mess in this place—wherever the filmmakers were. Like a recent war zone. Or a one-time construction site, abandoned for lack of funds. Lots of junk everywhere. Lots of heavy materials. Everything cooked in the sun.

Am I making this up?

The homeless Jesus guy kept being there, is my point—kept breaching the scene. And sometimes the frame would shift his way. Reposition on him.

So I had a good look.

He was the owner of a spiral notebook. Six by eight, I want to say. Also a pen. These things—his only things?—were pretty much always in use. He was writing and writing. Dude never quit writing, it seemed. Jesus diaper dude. With no thorns in his head. Though I want to add thorns, looking back.

Thorns in his head seems correct.

Anyway: For each word he wrote down (and he wrote without cease, he wrote without resting his hand), dude whispered. He spoke. He announced each syllable, and the syllables never stopped coming. He was some kind of genius. He'd gotten himself to the place where the words made themselves out of absences, out of needs that were barely perceived. Dude was some kind of genius. Writing in tongues, as it were. And I saw that. I saw how amazing he was, and how brilliant, how totally fucked. I saw my own self, kicking back, watching him on TV, Jesus diaper dude. And I felt—I don't know. I think I felt fortunate. Like I was clearly better off in every conceivable way.

Scott Garson is the author of the story collection *Is That You, John Wayne?* and *American Gymnopédies*, a collection of micro fictions. His work has won awards from *Playboy*, the Mary Roberts Rinehart Foundation, and Dzanc Books, and has been published by *American Short Fiction, The Kenyon Review, Conjunctions,* and many others. He lives in the American Midwest, where he teaches at the University of Missouri and edits the popular online flash fiction journal *Wigleaf*.

Frankie McMillan
The things we lose

[From *My Mother and the Hungarians, and other small fictions*
(Canterbury University Press, 2016)]

When she lost her keys or her cell phone, her bag or even her shoes and she was in a hurry to go somewhere she'd yell at him to help her. He'd look in the same bag she'd searched just a minute ago and find her car keys. Or he'd go to the pile of books on the table and straightaway find her cell phone. It made her light-headed. She'd kiss him madly. "How do you do it?" she'd exclaim. Only very rarely was he reluctant to look for her lost things and when she sensed that she'd offer him a reward. "Find my cell phone," she'd wink, "and I'll let loose all the horses. . . ."

She told him she was losing her marbles. Other people weren't always losing things. He said not to worry, he didn't mind looking; it was something he was good at.

She said she would tidy the house, it was the house swallowing up all the things, and for a week she tidied benches, tables, drawers, and bookshelves. Then one day she looked around and he was gone.

She lay alone in her upstairs bedroom staring up at the ceiling. There was a missing person in her house but how to call him, how to whistle him back she had no idea. Suddenly she sat up. Shouted out into the dark. "There'll be a reward," she cried.

Frankie McMillan is a New Zealand writer and poet. Her latest book *My Mother and the Hungarians, and other small fictions* was longlisted for the 2017 Ockham New Zealand Book Awards. In 2005, she was awarded the Creative New Zealand Todd New Writers' Bursary. Other awards include winner of the New Zealand Poetry Society International Poetry Competition in 2009 and winner of the New Zealand Flash Fiction Competition in 2013 and 2015. McMillan held the Ursula Bethell Residency in Creative Writing at the University of Canterbury in 2014, and in 2017 she was awarded the University of Auckland/Michael King writing residency.

Ras Mashramani :
Silent Hill

[From *Pank*, Issue 12, 2016]

There was a first generation Playstation video game about a young father who lost his child in a town where it snowed ash. Together you stumbled through foggy whiteness in the creature infested streets looking for her. Some early mornings you passed out in front of the living room TV screen watching hidden monsters behind your eyelids, ash in your hair, a fire burning forever underground. For so long it had been you and your father just like in the game running from stuccoed apartment to stuccoed apartment.

Except now there was a monster lingering over your living room, stinking up the brown rental carpeting, casting an inky shadow over the end of your sixth-grade year. And the monster was called disease, high blood pressure, cerebro-vascular accident, fallibility, mortality. And it was your father now who was lost in all that fog and whiteness, his speech garbled by stroke, dying in your living room. You played with your back to his hospital bed, this terror of a game, death behind you and in front of you, you beat the monsters down into bloody piles with two-by-fours and crow bars. Rarely shot anything, because bullets were spare and valuable.

You saved them for the bosses.

There was a 17-year-old across the way named Marquise who had a strong attraction to girls under 12 years old and the Sony Playstation franchise. You would sneak over the veranda to his apartment in the middle of the night. Together you killed the cursed dogs whose skin fell off as they ambled through the burnt snow, mannequins grotesquely animated— two plastic pelvises fused together, all legs and no head out of the shadows of the abandoned elementary school. Hiding in closets of empty apartments not unlike the one you inhabited in tangible life, watching demonic nonplayable characters enact sexual violence on one another, holding your breath for fear they would hear you through the screen.

You did this on the point of Marquise's knee, engrossed in game play, addicted to the focused labored attention of a teen-aged boy with sexual behavior issues and the fear of the screen, the fear of touch, wanting the fear, flattening all the affect and focusing it into this character, the Father, and his quest for his kid in this ghost town, and it was hard to disentangle Silent Hill from Paramount, California, and the neglected section 8 pool and automatic gates that made up the Sierra Gardens apartment complex.

It was hard to tell who you were when you played because you were lost in a game and you were lost in a lap and you were lost on the streets and in your house. Now you watch walk-throughs of the game when you can't sleep, revisiting the quiet town where you faced so many nightmares. You forgot about the boxy pixelation of the characters' bodies, or how tinny some of the Japanese gothcore music was coming through laptop speakers. But with the lights off, curled up in your bed, you are still there playing and being played.

Ras Mashramani is a Philadelphia-based, Net-reared function of the concrete utopia of Long Beach, California, and the deindustrialized

Ras Mashramani

West Indian refuge of Newark, New Jersey. She is a founding member of the corner store sci-fi and action collective, Metropolarity. Her collective's first book, *Style of Attack Report*, is a finalist for the 2017 Lambda Literary Award in science fiction. She is also a 2016 Leeway Foundation Art and Change Grant recipient.

Michael Hammerle :
Killerman

[From *Steel Toe Review*, Issue 25, 2016]

Cole got mad about what I'd said on the morning truck ride over to the job site, so Lance, the crew leader, put us on the same team. We had all been using scissor-lifts and concrete saws to cut and remove the ceiling of a museum. We would steady the slab on the top rail and lower each piece down. The two of us worked together all right that day—until lunch was called. We were coming down in the scissor-lift. Cole was at the yoke. He had his tinted safety glasses on and he looked at me with this clenched-jaw face and shook his head.

"You got a problem with me, man?" I said, putting my boot heel on the middle rail behind me. I had to grab the top rail to steady myself.

"I think you got a slick fuckin' mouth," he said as the basket locked in.

We unclipped our lanyards from their anchor points. I had to pass by him to get off the scissor-lift. I took that walk—hair up on my neck like a dog—and he rose up. Cole watched as I climbed out. I took off my harness, hung it on the rail, and made eye contact with him.

"I'm not your fuckin' homeboy," he said, when I had turned my back and got a few steps away. "I ain't with all this shit talking. You and Lance want to do that, that's fine. But you keep fucking with me and I'm gonna know something."

"I hear you. I still see you in that bucket, though," I said.

Cole is like an only child. He is down for laughs but if the jokes turn on him he gets pissed.

Our company had found Cole through Action Labor. He was in the work release program. He worked so well, the company had a job waiting for him when he was released from prison.

The morning Cole and I argued we had picked up a few workers from Action Labor. We had a short drive in the city before getting to the museum where we were working. The laborer who made it into the truck cabin had been talking my head off about baseball while Lance napped. Lance's body took up so much of the backseat that the man could not lean between the seats to talk—instead, he talked loud from the back. The laborer, at one point, slipped in that he needed a place to stay. I told him to stay at the Greensville Lodge. That's what pissed Cole off. Lance must have been sleeping lighter than I thought because he laughed.

"Yeah, Cole can recommend the lodge," said Lance.

I said the Greensville Lodge because it was fresh on my mind. Cole had recently told me that he stayed there. He said it was dirt cheap—a way to save up money when he first got out of prison.

After that day, we did not work together for a couple more days. I assumed Cole had talked to Lance about not wanting to work with me. Then Lance got us together at the shop to talk about the museum job. He said that we had left some bits of block in the ceiling-joints and because we were the last there we needed to remove them.

We took a truck to the museum and started to unload our tools. We hadn't spoken to each other yet. We were putting our harnesses on. Just before we were about to get into the scissor-lift, I said, "We don't have to be friends—like me or not—if something goes wrong I'm who's got your back and you've got mine. Feelings stay at home in the sock drawer."

"Naw, I'd let you fall," Cole said, and climbed in the lift.

I climbed in after him. "You ain't no killer, man." As soon as my feet were flat he was driving.

Cole and I, other than to discuss the job, didn't speak for the next three hours. By then we were almost finished. All that was left was a corner spot in the arch of the ceiling. Cole removed his last piece by standing on a middle rail and leaning his thighs into the top rail to steady himself.

I had to stand on the top rail. Cole actually looked worried. I grabbed the block—it wouldn't budge. I hit it a few times to break it up, but caulk was holding it together. I wound back, hard this time, and as I knocked the block free from the joint, I lost my balance. Cole grabbed my lanyard strap before I toppled over and he yanked me back into the basket. I came down on my backside. Cole had fallen down, too—although he was back on his feet standing at the yoke. I sat there breathing hard. He lowered the scissor-lift.

I got to my feet after the basket locked in. When my legs strengthened, I climbed out. I grabbed the debris cart and started collecting bits of the ceiling so I wouldn't have to acknowledge what happened.

Cole left the building, heading for the truck.

I could hear him talking on the phone. He was telling Lance that we'd be heading back to the shop soon. When he hung up, Cole came back into the room holding a push broom and a flat-shovel.

"Lance said, since it ain't three o'clock, he wants us to head over to Roy's job and help them remove a concrete wall they just cut an opening into."

"Yo, Cole," I said. He stopped shoveling block and looked at me. Cole no longer had that clenched jaw. He looked like himself again, but softer.

Michael Hammerle

Michael Hammerle holds a BA in English, cum laude, from the University of Florida. His prose has been published in the *Steel Toe Review* and the *Matador Review*. His poetry has appeared in *Eunoia Review*, *Mosaic Art & Literary Journal*, and *Poetry Quarterly*, where his poem was a contender for the 2016 Rebecca Lard Award. Hammerle was named a finalist for the 2016 *Hayden's Ferry Review* Flash Fiction Contest and for Press 53's 2015 *Prime Number Magazine* Awards. He lives near Gainesville, Florida.

Gen Del Raye :
The Truth About Distance

[From *wildness*, Issue No. 4, June 2016]

Either you are there or you are not. There is no "close." For example, when I was ten the biggest earthquake in anyone's memory hit two hours away from my house. On the television screen there were elevated highways lying on their sides like resting greyhounds, buildings fallen face first in the dirt. At my house the little aquarium in the kitchen sloshed half its water onto the floor. I was asleep on the carpet. By the time my mother dragged me under the table, it was over.

Or here's another one. Once I was at the beach when a little boy drowned. They said he didn't know how to swim out of the riptide. They said his parents ran up and down the beach, calling his name, looking for his arms to reach above the waves. And what did I see? Afterward, on the drive home, a little splash, a hint of skin.

Or take my dog. If ever there was an animal that knew the truth about distance, it would have been that dog. Quiet nights sitting together on the carpet, my mother reading a book while my father and I played chess, the dog would arrange his body so as to touch a part of all of us. His nose against my knee, left forefoot against my father's back, right hindfoot against my mother's toes. If you wanted to, if you were feeling mean, you could slowly move away from him, inch by inch, so that even in his sleep he would stretch out further and further, like a prisoner on a rack.

Or else the nights when there were thunderstorms or fireworks from the lake. My dog with his wide eyes flitting between us, whining whenever one of us got up to use the bathroom or otherwise moved out of his anxious reach.

The month before I went away, I got a lot of advice. Such as—

My cousin, pinching the skin around my stomach: Don't eat too many burgers and fries over there.

My uncle: Don't get shot. He says this seriously. Says something about a kid in Texas a few years ago who knocked on someone's door just to ask for directions and got blown to pieces by a double-barreled shotgun. It's legal, my uncle said, to blow people apart in America with a double-barreled shotgun if they are standing at your front door. Don't knock unless it's someone you trust.

My aunt: Don't forget us. Even though I know it's expensive to call I promise we'll try not to talk too long so you won't go broke. This is when I explain to her about Skype. I say I promise to call if she promises to set up an account so it will be free. I say distance isn't as big a problem these days as it used to be.

Let's not exaggerate. Let's not pretend a little scratch is a lasting wound. Seat 29B on UA35 somewhere above the Marshall Islands. To the right of me is an old man asleep against the window. To the left is a girl with her bare feet flush against the seatback in front of her. Before me is the latest release of *Fast and Furious*, or maybe it's *Godzilla*, or *The Parent Trap*. Nothing is happening anywhere else. I am missing nothing.

But before I board the plane, when I am still waiting at the gate and I get a call from an impossible number, something like 08100540001, I feel my stomach churn.

Distance. Someday my parents will die, or my friends will die, and I won't be there. Late nights, calling home and listening to the ring tone go on and on, that's what I think.

Gen Del Raye was born and raised in Kyoto, Japan. His stories have appeared in *Booth, The Monarch Review, NANO Fiction,* and elsewhere. He was named a finalist for the *Glimmer Train* Short Story Award for New Writers, a semifinalist for the American Short(er) Fiction Contest, was nominated for the *Best of the Net* anthology, and is a recipient of the Inkslinger Award from *Buffalo Almanack*. He is currently getting his MFA at San Francisco State University.

Cameron Quincy Todd
We Are All Relatively Safe Here

[From *Inch*, No. 31, Summer 2016]

My sister and the bunnies arrived on the same day. Frannie, at dawn, off the bus from West Baltimore, seven months along. The baby rabbits, after mass, on the church lawn in a yellow basket, needing homes. It was the week after Easter.

From the front window, my younger sisters and I watched Frannie come home. She carried her weight awkwardly. She was too thin, anemic. Her curls formed a shadowy halo against the neon sign hanging from the Adolfis' house next door: an open hand, the words *PSYCHIC READINGS: PALM & TAROT*, and, in the center of the hand, *$10*.

After church my mother bought hamburger meat, frozen fish, and chewy vitamins that tasted like chocolate. For the rabbits she bought iceberg lettuce, carrot sticks.

"They stay outside," she said, and we nodded. We'd never had a pet.

That week, in the neighborhood, we were talked about. We had a scandal, and we had bunnies. No one was more jealous than the Adolfi children, who watched us through the triangle-shaped hole in the fence as we set up a crate in the yard and lined it with old *Baltimore Suns*. My younger sisters had questions: Do rabbits eat meat? Will they go to heaven?

The next Sunday, at lunch, we tried not to look as Frannie took piece after piece of meat in her mouth, rolled it around against her tongue, and spat it out. She was still at the table, staring into her plate, when the little ones ran in from the yard to announce that the bunnies were gone. They were too small, too sleepy to have escaped. There was no sign of forced entry. There was only the rip in the back fence, large enough for a small child to shimmy through.

Mrs. Adolfi opened the door to our brood, on her steps, for the first and only time. She sized up my mother. Both women, arms crossed, Mrs. Adolfi taller, wearing dark eyeliner that would have looked beautiful on my mother.

"Where are the fucking rabbits?" said my mother. For a moment we looked around to see where the words could have come from.

Inside, the house was dark, velvety. No crystal ball, but also no television, no toys. Stacks of dusty books, magazines. Strange cards spread out along the table: the fool, the magician. A heart full of daggers. The smell of wet dirt, and something sanguine cooking on the stove, maybe beets. No one spoke. And then we saw them.

There were as many of them, the children, as there were of us, but they were smaller, with skinny arms and pale skin, almost blue. They watched us with round eyes, bunnies covering their bodies, hanging from their arms and shoulders. Draped in fur, they resembled a portrait of a royal family from a cold, long-away empire.

A little Adolfi girl spoke first, her voice high and crackling. "The boys did it," she said, and the three women nodded.

The transfer was slow and silent. Soon our shirts were stuffed with the animals; even my mother held one. We filed out. We'd gotten what we'd come for.

But Frannie hung back, and from the doorway I watched her hold out her hands to Mrs. Adolfi, the mass of her pregnancy between them. Then she turned them over, revealing her palms, white and glistening with sweat.

"Please," Frannie said. "Tell me something. Anything."

After some time, Mrs. Adolfi said, "Even the animal knows what is essential." Her hair, a brilliant dark tangle of braids, seemed to vibrate. She brought a hand to her head and began to pull, as if unraveling a ball of yarn. She held it out: one bunny, left behind. She placed it in Frannie's palms.

"We all die. Meanwhile, we survive."

We watched the rabbit twitch and settle.

In a month, Frannie would deliver a purple, screaming boy. She would divorce, and the Church wouldn't forgive us. When the baby cried for a week straight, a tinted glass bottle would arrive at our door, with a note that said *apply twice daily*. The salve would smell like twigs and some other earthiness, and it would cure him.

That afternoon, while Mrs. Adolfi passed her hands along the small rabbit, I swear I could feel his warmth, hear his tiny heartbeat.

"Anything else is ten dollars," she said.

Cameron Quincy Todd is a graduate of Colorado College and the MFA Program at the University of New Orleans. Her work has appeared in *Inch, HOUSEGUEST Magazine,* and *ROAR.* She is the recipient of the 2014 Samuel Mockbee Award in Nonfiction, and of scholarships from the Prague Summer Writing Program, the University of New Orleans, and the New York State Summer Writer's Institute. She currently lives in New Orleans, where she writes about travel and culture for *Fodor's Travel*, and is at work on a novel.

Mona Leigh Rose
The Crossing

[From *The Writing Disorder*, Winter 2016]

Ricardo says you cannot hear them. They slink like cats, he says. Ricardo says you cannot see them, not like you'd see your sister waiting on the curb for the school bus. They're in the shadows, he says. That flick in the corner of your eye? That's them, he says. When you see that flick, if you turn fast enough you might see the tip of a shoe or a wisp of hair. When you see that flick, you must move closer, you must look behind the utility box, around the block wall, deep into the shadows. If you ignore that flick, she will wait, not moving, not breathing. She will wait for the train and then, when it's too late, you'll see her. You'll see her slide her body onto the tracks, under the crushing wheels, silently, skillfully, as if she's been practicing all her life for this act. She will reveal herself at the last possible moment, right as the train is passing, right as her life is ending, right as your life is beginning. And then you'll be fired.

That's how it happened for Ricardo. He worked security at this crossing for seven months. Seven months of watching and waiting, seven months of double-time pay, seven months of being a man. Then the teenage girl crept out of the shadows and ended it all. Now he works at fast food for minimum wage. No other boss will hire him. He is dirty, tainted with her blood.

Now he wakes up in the middle of the night, soaked in sweat, replaying that day, wondering if there was a flick, wondering if he could have stopped her, wondering if he will ever be a man again.

I took over Ricardo's shift after the accident. Now I watch for girls who don't want to be seen, listen for boys who don't want to be heard. Teenagers who want to end their lives before they begin.

Every time it happens, the people and the newspapers tell us who, they tell us why: Parents who sacrifice everything so their children can have better lives. Parents who expect the impossible. Parents who are themselves geniuses, over-achievers, the smartest in the world, who expect their children to do better. Children who grow up on the edge of the University, surrounded by the children of the smartest people in the world, who are told that if they don't do better, they're nothing. Children who sit in classrooms and libraries and tutoring centers under florescent lights for ten hours a day since they were three. Teenagers who go to the funerals of other teenagers who slid under the train. Young men and women who can think of no other option than to lie down under steel wheels to end the humiliation, the shame, of not getting into Harvard, of not scoring a perfect 2400 on their SATs, of not doing better than the smartest people in the world.

I know the older brothers of these kids. I played against them on the soccer pitch, rich against poor. I saw them around the edges of their town, when they crossed into my town. They wouldn't talk to me, wouldn't see me, wouldn't hear me. Now their younger brothers and sisters dive below the trains. They still don't talk to me or see me, but I'm the one who will save their families.

Mr. Johanson says the worst is around finals, and the worst of the worst is when college admissions go out in the spring. That's when they come to the tracks, he says. That's when you must be extra alert, he says. That's also when the loud ones, the strange ones, come down to the crossing, sit on the block wall and watch. They think it's sport, or a movie, or something to Tweet about. They think it's funny to place bets with their allowance money. Those ones are easy to see, easy to hear. I chase them away. They laugh at me. They don't understand.

The commuter trains, they slow at the crossing. I see the faces of the conductors as they pass. Their mouths tighten, their eyes dart, the creases on their foreheads deepen with each pass. The freight trains, they don't slow. Their cars and TVs and cattle are too important, must reach the markets. I don't see the faces of those conductors. Do they see me? Do they understand?

My grandfather, he doesn't understand. "*Los trenes trajo vida a mi pueblo,*" he says. "*Los trenes eran nuestra esperanza, nuestra manera de entrar a América,*" he says. He and his friends also waited in the shadows beside the tracks. They also crept silently toward the fast-moving trains. But they jumped onto the trains, they prayed to escape the crush of the steel wheels, they pulled each other onto the train cars and hid from the conductors. They rode the trains to freedom, to jobs, to a better life.

My brothers, they don't understand. "You're a crossing guard for spoiled rich kids," they say. "Yes," I say. "A crossing guard for spoiled rich kids who makes twice what you make." That quiets them down.

My mother, she understands. "You are doing good, Joselito," she says. "You are helping the sad *niños*, you are becoming *un buen hombre*. You are doing good." "Yes," I say to my mother. "I am doing good, and I will become a man."

Mr. Johanson also says that I'm doing good. He says that I'll be promoted, will be a supervisor, will stop watching for children who don't want to be seen and will be the boss of other men. But first, I must see the flick. I must look deep into the shadows. I must be a man.

Mona Leigh Rose is infatuated with short stories, the shorter the better. Her fiction has appeared in *Avalon Literary Review, The Writing Disorder,* and *Luna Review.* She lives and writes in Santa Barbara, California.

Emily Corwin

Bildungsroman

after Sonya Vatomsky

[From *Cease, Cows*, June 2016]

If you come upon a fire, trembling still with bark and pine cones, almost out, you go by. If you come upon a rustling, a pair of eyes blinking back, you go by. You go by because this is the woods and you know what happens to little girls, skipping into the brush with wicker baskets and clean socks. You listened to your mother—you are very good. You thought it best to avoid the woods altogether, only watching the trees crackle darkly from your bedroom window.

You recall when autumn came, when you were nearly not a girl—that's when the butter knives vanished, one by one over the golden months. Soon there was only one knife to share between you and Mother, passed back and forth, edge slick in yellow. She suspected you of mischief. When that last one departed—gone in the night—she sent you to bed, no supper. Soon it was all the silverware. Then a candlestick, a tablecloth, a white dress that was drying on the clothesline. All disappeared without a trace.

Mother grew quieter and days grew shorter, on the edge of snow. She no longer asked you about the silver. You began to suspect something sinister: claw marks on the door, flowers trampled in the garden, footprints leading from the house to the woods. Something stealing from you in the night. Something scraping up and down the hall, and by morning, Mother too was gone, an empty chair in the kitchen.

You decided it was time to be brave. So it's into the trees, following her scent—gardenia, wax, butter. And if now, at last, if you come upon a house made of sticks, smoke twining upward, your own dress drying from a branch in the yard, be quiet and quick, little one. You know what can happen.

Emily Corwin is an MFA candidate in poetry at Indiana University–Bloomington and the poetry editor for *Indiana Review*. Her writing has appeared in *Gigantic Sequins, Painted Bride Quarterly, Hobart, smoking glue gun,* and *Word Riot*. She has two chapbooks, *My Tall Handsome* (Brain Mill Press) and *darkling* (Platypus Press), which were both published in 2016.

W. Todd Kaneko
Metalhead's Pledge

[From *New South*, March 7, 2016]

From the rear wall, Metalhead looks at the back of a girl's head in history class. She is the only black girl in class and always sits in front, right next to the American flag. They are learning about Civil Rights, how one man had a dream and taught America about the content of a person's character. Metalhead thinks about how he hasn't said the Pledge of Allegiance since second grade—he just mouths the words to a song he once sang with his father on a car trip to Saginaw about dragons and smoking grass. After class, Metalhead will eat a slice of pizza and get high in the back parking lot. After school, his father won't discuss layoffs at the auto plant, and when the family moves to a more remote suburb, there will be no conversation about white flight or a neighborhood's changing hues as it breaks and corrodes. He won't ask why his friends play air guitar along with Eddie Van Halen and Jimmy Page but never Jimi Hendrix because one day he will sell used cars and a woman he remembers from high school will ask to take a rickety Ford Tempo for a test drive. He won't remember her name, but will recall how she once looked at him that way a child looks at an injured animal before learning that people aren't supposed to reveal how they feel inside. He won't let her drive the Tempo, guiding her to a car with a sturdier axle, a truthful odometer. This will happen decades after that girl in the front row looks back at the clock ticking over Metalhead's desk. Her eyes fall on him for a moment before she turns back around. Metalhead places his hand on his heart and discovers it still beating.

W. Todd Kaneko is author of *The Dead Wrestler Elegies* (Curbside Splendor, 2014) and coauthor of the forthcoming *Poetry: A Writer's Guide and Anthology* (Bloomsbury Academic, 2018). His poems and prose have appeared in *Bellingham Review*, *Los Angeles Review*, *The Normal School*, *NANO Fiction*, *SmokeLong Quarterly*, *Barrelhouse*, and many other journals and anthologies. A Kundiman fellow, he is coeditor of the online literary magazine *Waxwing* and lives in Grand Rapids, Michigan, where he teaches at Grand Valley State University.

Matthew Baker :
The President's Doubles

[From *Booth*, February 2016]

The president of the island had been president for nearly nineteen years, and, as was often the case with presidents, many people wanted to kill the president, and some people even had threatened to, and some people even had attempted to, which was why, nineteen years earlier, before the president had even been sworn into office, the president's advisers had begun searching the island for lookalikes. The president's advisers insisted that the president have doubles. The president was against having doubles. The president's appearance wasn't exactly common or uncommon—beady eyes, a broad nose, full lips, a constellation of moles across the neck. Lookalikes were found. A bank clerk. A mail carrier. A rice farmer. Others. The president's surgeons reshaped their faces, altered their bodies, tweaked their hairlines, however necessary, and after that the bank clerk and the mail carrier and the rice farmer and the others lived at the president's mansion, and wore the president's suits, and dined at the president's table, with the president. Every day, the president and the doubles would leave the mansion together, lower themselves into separate sedans with separate drivers, and get driven to separate meetings. The president wasn't convinced that the doubles were necessary. That first year of the presidency, a double was being driven through the city when an anarchist fired a missile at the sedan, totaling the sedan and killing the double. The president didn't know whether the double killed had been the former bank clerk, the former mail carrier, the former rice farmer, or whoever, but regardless, after that the president was convinced that the doubles were necessary. As was often the case with presidents, the president wanted to avoid assassination. The president had vowed to reform the island, which the president loved. The president often paced the president's office, brooding about the island's past, worrying about the island's future. The president had been born in a hut in the island's capital, had been scarred across the shins by the island's reefs as a child, had been educated as an adult by the island's universities. The doubles, now, had scars across their shins. Sometimes the doubles would appear at official functions, as the president, and would have to give speeches, and make promises, and cast votes on certain issues. That wasn't a problem. The president wrote the speeches the doubles gave, and chose the promises the doubles made, and instructed the doubles how to vote. Whatever the president said, the doubles did. During the fifth year of the presidency, a double was poisoned with a lemon tart. Also the fifth year of the presidency, a double was poisoned with a milk tea. Also the fifth year of the presidency, a double was poisoned with a tube of toothpaste. The doubles always spoke with the president's voice, as the doubles had been trained to speak—pronouncing how the president pronounced, enunciating how the president enunciated, speaking at the president's pitch. The seventh year of the presidency, a double was watching a ballet from a private box at the national theater when an anarchist disguised as an attendant stabbed the double thirteen times with a switchblade stiletto. As the double coughed blood onto the rich carpeting of the private box, the double, in the president's voice, spoke the double's dying words. Only the anarchist overheard the double's dying words. Moments later that anarchist was killed. The island's healthcare system was improving, the island's crime rate was decreasing, the island's economy had recovered from a recession, but nevertheless that ninth year of the presidency the president was shot in the neck while giving a speech at a rally. The president survived, but just barely. After that the president and the doubles were moved from the mansion to a building like a fortress—concrete walls, barred windows—and the doubles themselves were given doubles. Every day, a double and that double's doubles would leave the fortress together, lower themselves into separate sedans with separate drivers, and get driven to separate meetings. Then another double and that double's doubles would leave the fortress together, and then another double and that double's doubles would leave the fortress together, and then another double and that double's doubles would leave the fortress together. Every few months the anarchists would manage to kill a double, or a double's double, trying to kill the president, but what the anarchists didn't know was that the president never left the fortress. The president's advisers insisted that the president never leave the fortress. The doubles and the doubles' doubles appeared as the president, wherever the president needed to appear, whenever the president needed to appear. The president had the mind the island needed; the doubles and the doubles' doubles had the bodies. Sometime in the fifteenth year of the presidency, the president's advisers thought of a troubling possibility: What if the anarchists themselves made a double, sent the fake double to the fortress, and had the fake double kill the president? After that the doubles and the doubles' doubles were given separate houses on the island, and nobody was allowed into the fortress, except for the president, who lived there, and a blind servant, who lived there, who cooked the president's meals and washed the president's clothes and cleaned the president's rooms. Deliveries were left at the door. All communication was done over computer. Years passed, and as various doubles were shot, and bombed, and stabbed, and strangled, and poisoned, and bludgeoned, security at the fortress became increasingly heightened—fences were built around the fortress, and guards patrolled the fortress, and rumors were spread that the fortress was now a prison, to mislead the anarchists, but the truth is that it was a prison, that the president lived like a prisoner, that the president ate meals from a tray, and wore the same clothes day after day, and at night often stared out the window of the office, watching the guards on the watchtowers, dreaming of escaping.

Matthew Baker is the author of *If You Find This*, a Booklist Top Ten Debut of 2015 and an Edgar Award Nominee for 2016, and his stories have appeared in publications such as *American Short Fiction, New England Review, One Story, Electric Literature, Conjunctions,* and *Best of the Net.* A recipient of grants and fellowships from organizations including the Fulbright Commission, the MacDowell Colony, the Whiting Foundation, the Ucross Foundation, the Ragdale Foundation, and the Bread Loaf Writers' Conference, he has an MFA from Vanderbilt University, where he was the founding editor of *Nashville Review.* He was born and lives in Michigan.

Jesse Goolsby
Waist Deep at Hapuna

[From *Pleiades* 36.2, Summer 2016]

I was sixteen, newly licensed, and I couldn't fool the cop after five shots of Black Bear whiskey, so why try? By the time Mom picked me up at the Hilo jail, I was mostly sober and unafraid. It wasn't the first time I'd been there. As a kid you're always told that jail is the worst place on Earth, but that isn't true, not by a long shot. Google Alzheimer's or Jaycee Dugard.

Mom wore a *Fuck Cancer* T-shirt and a misaligned wig. She'd named me after herself, so when the deputy called out "Marie" we both said, "What?" We drove home listening to the Deftones album I loved. I didn't know if she had the strength to lecture or beat me, so I paid my respects by staying quiet as we passed over the Wailuku River. Our empty driveway shouldn't have surprised me, but it did, just as it had for the year since Dad left for the hellhole that is Sacramento. Later, as I showered, I wondered if I would have to live with him and his fat girlfriend if Mom died before my eighteenth birthday. But I knew there was a good chance no one would care where I went.

Way too early that morning Mom came into my bedroom and turned on the lights. She wasn't impulsive, so it scared the crap out of me. She wore her UC Davis shorts from her old days, and she made me look at the new scars where her breasts used to be. She held a white belt in her hand, and she stood there for five minutes, her arms at her sides. I thought she would hit me or make me touch her, so I cowered and begged her to go away.

"Do you want to look like this?" she said.

"No," I said.

"This is where you're headed."

I was afraid and confused, and why not? When I glanced at the motionless ceiling fan Mom said, "No. Here," and pointed at her chest.

Her scars looked like pink smiles, and I could see purple veins through her skin. The color had drained from her face, and she looked down at herself and grimaced. Her legs were long and toned because she worked out like crazy through chemo, as if she was still her eighteen-year-old volley-ball-player self. Fanaticism, maybe, but it's better than daytime soap operas and a liter of Coke. But Mom's upper half? It was no longer hers, at least that's what I read in her horror.

"You drink again and I'll kill you," she said. She was still staring at her body. If it had been any other time or place I would have laughed. Mom never carried through with threats. That's what I hated about her.

Before she turned and left she said our name, but how was I to know if she was talking to me?

Although I didn't think about it that morning, I've often wondered if you can recover from genuine loneliness, and each time I convince myself that the answer is yes. Sure, I've seen sane people jump from the Golden Gate. I've heard stories about one-legged vets hanging themselves in closets, or people catching Alzheimer's in their forties. I've put down a pint of Black Bear on a Tuesday night, all alone. All of it is horrible

Jesse Goolsby

shit, but I remember the Monday my dad's Jeep returned to our driveway in Hilo. He came through the door with fried chicken and sat down like it was nothing. I've waded into the calm ocean at Hapuna with Mom and held her weightless body in my arms. I've seen her yellow bikini stuck to her flat chest, how the whole damn beach noticed. Fuck them and their pathetic whispers. Mom walked me down the goddamn aisle, and you still think there's sanctity in our bodies?

Jesse Goolsby is the author of the novel *I'd Walk with My Friends If I Could Find Them* (Houghton Mifflin Harcourt), winner of the Florida Book Award for Fiction and long-listed for the Flaherty-Duncan First Novel Prize. His fiction and essays have appeared widely in journals, including *Narrative Magazine, Kenyon Review, Epoch, Salon,* and have appeared in or been recognized by the *Best American* series. He is the recipient of the Richard Bausch Fiction Prize, the John Gardner Memorial Award in Fiction, and fellowships from the Sewanee Writers' Conference and the Hambidge Center for Creative Arts and Sciences. He earned a PhD in English from Florida State University, and lives in Colorado Springs, Colorado.

Alvin Park :

tree rot

[From *wildness*, Issue No. 6, October 2016]

On this day, when the sun picked through the clouds, the trees shed their skin like paper. The men and women in town called it disease, called it the devil's touch. They said, Our forest will be undone by this fungus, this airborne rot.

To tell them of my wife who did the taking. To tell them how she gathered the leaves, already stronger than the limbs that once held them. The bark peeling and the knife cutting away the precious meat. How she stirred them into broth and drank deep.

I wanted to say, The taking of the trees has stopped the disease in her, has rebuilt her immunities, kept her veins from coming undone. See the color in her cheeks. See how red her lips. See how we've learned to kiss again, to sweat, to place mouth to shoulder and collarbone.

I brushed my hand across the oak that stood outside our home and came away with bark of ash and dirt, my fingers digging inches into the tree's belly.

The felling, the crumbling as birds and squirrels and termites choked on that powder. She buried those cold bodies in the dirt, by the roots that dried and fell fallow and impotent.

She said, We can hope the trees can feed and grow anew on fur and bone and carapace.

But each morning, seeing more of the trees cleared, bent backward by their own desiccating spines, buckling knees. The crops thinning, ribs tucked between fragile leaf and unseeded fruit.

The townspeople filled their wagons, set their eyes to some new plain. They said, The trees will be gone soon and the land will go with it.

Meaning she would run out soon. Meaning her body would rebel again, awaking to retching, her bones hollowing. Meaning we would have to abandon this land just like them, find some new trees to brew her elixirs, new forests to take from, to uproot.

Each morning we stood at our porch and saw more of the hills once hidden, once paled by the heads of trees. She dreamed of the staying we could do, the family we hoped to raise.

I want to teach our children of those hills, she said, I want to build a home.

How I wished to give her everything, every blood and bone and potion. How I wished the land a desert to have her whole again.

Alvin Park lives and writes in Portland, Oregon. Some of his publication credits include *The Rumpus, Mojave River Review, Alice Blue Review, Wyvern Lit, Synaesthesia Magazine, New South Journal, wildness,* and *SmokeLong Quarterly.* He is associate fiction editor at the online literary magazine *Little Fiction.*

Keith Woodruff
Summer

[From *Quarter After Eight*, Issue 22, 2016]

We were a storm. Five boys smashing through fields and fences with a tornado's rage, ripping down every "no trespassing" sign in sight. The countryside was ours. Birds held in their song as we passed; even the grass bowed down flat. Nights, we'd sneak out bedroom windows, crushing cricket song under foot as we prowled from house to house to steal from porches, to peek in windows, our hearts beating loud as the moon was bright. Days, we'd walk the Grand River, spearing it dry of carp with homemade spears and leaving their bodies to rot on the river's edge. We should have left Crazy Bob there, too. But even though he dug out a carp's eyes with his fingers and threw it back to see if it could swim blind, we kept him. Even though he laughed hysterically when it simply sank, we kept him. For without us, he'd be home with a dad who was all beers and fists and even bit him once. Like a pack, we'd run through the swamp grass and spook up deer that had bedded down, chase them on foot—sure we'd catch one with our bare hands when the wind at our backs was enough to grant us predator foot speed. When the deer were no longer enough, we turned on each other with pellet guns, flushing the silence up in flocks from acres of sleeping fields with our screams and

115

Keith Woodruff

warrior pantomimes, small bursts of murderous play that left us bleeding but still friends, and for that, nailed up like stars in each other's minds.

Keith Woodruff was born in San Jose, California. He has a Masters in Poetry/Creative Writing from Purdue University and lives in Akron, Ohio. His work has appeared in *Poetry East, Zone 3, Tar River Poetry, American Literary Review, Quarter After Eight, The Journal, Painted Bride Quarterly,* and *Wigleaf.* He is a *Best of the Net* and Pushcart Prize nominee.

Oscar Mancinas :
Tourista

[From *The Tishman Review*, Vol. 2, Issue 4, 2016]

I'd gone out drinking the night before even though it was a Tuesday and I had class the following day at 10 a.m., so I was asleep when the phone rang at about 3 p.m. and I stumbled over to where my roommate and I had put the landline in our dorm room and answered *Huh?* and from the other side heard *Is Ernesto there?* and still didn't know what was going on so I grunted and the voice said, *This is Mark in the admissions office, we have a student and his father who want a tour of the campus,* and I recognized the words but still wasn't sure what was happening because I didn't work for the admissions office, had never taken a tour, and had only been a student for two months, so I looked out the window at the New England fall foliage—which still felt new—to corroborate this, but, somehow, I said *Uh-huh* and Mark, who may've been a student or just another person from Maine working for the wealthy private college in town, said, *Well, they're Mexican, and they want a Mexican tour guide, and* (I'm not excluding any part of what Mark said, he stopped himself before uttering the fact that'd slapped me in the face when I first got to campus: there are no Mexicans—or, there weren't; I guess people like Mark could now say, *Yes, we have someone who we can call up, just a minute, please*), so maybe it was because I missed my family, missed my hood in El Valle, missed Arizona, or maybe it was some sense of obligation to the school, which had funded my escape from those things, or maybe I was just a down, hungover teenager looking for company, but I said, *Yeah, I'll head over*, hung up the phone, walked to the bathroom down the hall, washed my face, and left my dorm in the direction of the first Mexican people I'd seen in months, who were, when I got there, as advertised, a father and son—both unmistakably brown but definitely whiter than I'd pictured, but our hair and eyes could be traded and no one would know the difference— and they smiled when they saw me, said, *Hello nice to meet you*, and then *un placer* once I let them know I was the kind of Mexican-American who spoke Spanish, not just the cholo Spanglish but the type of Spanish professors cared about, the type of Spanish (I've since learned) necessary in airports, for going through customs, but nowhere else in Latin America or Spain or even the U.S., but I didn't know this then, so when the father (whose name I've since forgotten) said, *Órale, vámonos en nuestro tour*, I laughed out of familiarity and unease, and we began our tour by walking to the Student Union and then to the humanities building, which I knew the most about but also knew next to nothing about because, like I said, it was my first semester in college and I hadn't learned enough to tell anyone why it was better or worse than any other college; I wasn't even sure whether it was better than the hood—no, it was definitely better than the hood, but I couldn't say why— and, anyway, Jonas (that was the kid's name) was interested in doing something pre-med, so *Can we go to the sciences building?* his dad said after a short while, and on the walk across the quad, where I pointed up the hill to the library and said *biblioteca* and waited for both of them to acknowledge my tour guide action, Jonas's dad asked, *Y qué onda con las chicas?* with his head tilted down, eyes looking over glasses, as a group of white girls (definitely upperclassmen) walked past us, and I laughed to show I understood and said, *Lotsa really smart, pretty girls here*, and Jonas's dad nudged Jonas with the back of his hand and wheeze-laughed while Jonas smiled and turned crimson, then we were at the science building—a place I'd never been, so didn't say much about—and we walked past classes and labs before sitting in one of the lounges and talking about other things: *Naciste en México?* Jonas's dad asked and I told him I hadn't been but both of my parents had, *Y de dónde son tus padres?* he asked and I said, *Mi Amá es de Monterrey, Nuevo León*, to which he nodded, approving, and said, *One of my sisters lives there, ciudad magnífica!* and I smiled and said, *And mi Apá es de Cajeme, Sonora*, and his smile disappeared into his face, like a window slamming shut, but he managed to say, *Never spent much time in Sonora, too much happening there*, and Jonas looked at the ground, so I said, *You should! My Apá's people, los Yaquis, treat turistas well and cook great food*, but no one spoke, so my words hit the floor like trash in a bag, and I sat there and thought maybe I'd given the wrong answer or given the right one without showing work, like I'd cheated or something, but I hadn't and I tried to tell myself I wasn't embarrassed and didn't care what they thought, so I said I had to get back to work and it was good getting to know them, I wished Jonas luck on picking a college because I felt like we hadn't really talked and he seemed like a genuinely nice kid, and his dad shook my hand professionally, disinterested, and said, *Muchas gracias, muchacho*, and I nodded the way I would to a stranger—an older one expecting nothing from me or my kind—and walked back to my dorm thinking about Amá and Apá and the weight of their hometowns, the enormity of which dried my mouth with fear, so I texted a friend to see where there would be beer that night and awaited the oncoming darkness.

Oscar Mancinas is the proud son of Mexican immigrants. Hailing from Mesa, Arizona, he is currently completing an MFA in creative writing at Emerson College and will soon begin work as a PhD candidate in Transborder Studies at Arizona State University. His fiction can be found at *Queen Mob's Teahouse, 3Elements Review,* and *Cosmonauts Avenue.* His poetry can be found, or is forthcoming, in *Blue Mesa Review, Hayden's Ferry Review,* and *Rising Phoenix Review.*

Cole Meyer :
Nightstands

[From *SmokeLong Quarterly*, Issue Fifty-Three, September 2016]

Every morning I wake with a new woman on my left. Every morning I wake with my wife on the right, and I expect her to be yelling, to be angry, demanding to know why I've been unfaithful, but every morning she is only ashes in an urn. Dust collects on the nightstand so I know she hasn't emerged in the night, hasn't taken one look at the woman in her place and stormed off. I wonder, now, when this woman will leave. I think about making her pancakes, about sprinkling my wife on top so this woman will become a little more like her. Maybe she will take her hair color, her name. Maybe she will absorb her memories, absorb everything but her breasts and she will be my wife, and healthy. I mark a tally through the dust, one for every night I should've slept alone.

Cole Meyer studied creative writing and classical humanities at the University of Wisconsin–Madison. He reviews books for *The Masters Review*, and his writing appears or is forthcoming at *SmokeLong*

Cole Meyer

Quarterly, The Citron Review, SAND, and elsewhere. He lives in Saint Paul and works in IT at the University of Minnesota–Twin Cities. He Tweets about writing and baseball.

Lydia Armstrong : The November We Are Fifteen

[From *Neon Literary Magazine*, Issue 43, 2016]

The November we are fifteen we run away and the boys around the block put us up in a motel room on the turnpike that has a hole in the door so we can see everyone's sneakers shuffling past.

We write poetry and eat potato chips all week and one night I sit on the chipped-tile bathroom floor and feel my mind break apart and the pieces get sucked up into the air vent.

On Thanksgiving the Arab at the front desk calls and says in broken English no one's paid the bill for the night but we understand clearly when he says, *I'm calling police.*

We hide our bags in the woods and use the last of our change to call the boys from the pay phone at Waffle House and the ringing just trills through the ear piece like a jungle bird.

We tell the waiter behind the counter we don't have money and he watches us the way my father looks at sick dogs.

Lydia Armstrong :

After an hour he gives us coffee and after two hours he goes over to the gas station and buys us cigarettes and after three hours he puts sopping plates of smothered hash browns in front of us that we can't eat.

Two boys with slick white smiles and a car say we can go with them and the waiter behind the counter keeps wiping the same spot and watches us go out into the dawn, where everything is soft and blue at the edges and we are glad the night has passed.

The slick boys have keys to an uncle's barber shop and say, here sit on our laps, and we look at each other like maybe this is exciting, maybe something is happening.

Something must be happening because the lights are off but the room is still glowing and the only thing holding us onto these bony knees are the arms slung over our hips.

But it's hard to tell because we are weak from hunger and sleeplessness and the blunt passing through our hands and all we want is home.

The problem with a strange boy's lap at dawn is that it shrinks your hearts, like how eating potato chips for a week shrinks your stomach, and when someone tries to give you something real, there isn't anywhere to put it.

Lydia Armstrong lives in Richmond, Virginia. Her work has appeared in *The Bitchin' Kitsch, Apt, Arsenic Lobster, The Axe Factory, Blotter-ature, Rogue Poetry, FIVE:2:ONE* magazine, and *Crack the Spine,* where "The November We Are Fifteen" first appeared in 2016. Her poem "The Doctor" has been nominated for the Forward Prize in England for Best Single Poem. She is currently working on a novel.

Erin Calabria :
The Last Fragile Thing

[From *Third Point Press*, Issue 4, 2016]

I knew he was going to leave even before that winter, the air stitched with sleet while the two of us led the horses back and forth from old Hugh's stable down a washed-out road, our feet freezing in boots lined with plastic bags until spring came and we mucked the stalls of shit caked gold and steaming almost to our knees, which was how old Hugh liked it in the cold, claiming it kept his ancient spindle of a pony warm, not that we'd had any choice of course, not for nearly a year since our father's barn burned to the ground, smoke gushing thick like a wound that can't be staunched, black and more black tumbling over the trees, the neighbors calling at first to see if only the sugarhouse might've gone up, a chimney burn, a fallen nest, until the whole town gathered in the yard, crushing down all the new grass just sprouted through grains of thawing snow, since by then there was nothing to do but watch, though no one ever knew whether it was a spark from the evaporator fire flown up into the loft, or whether it was that uncanny alchemy of hay cut in sunshine but baled after a storm, the way tiny cells trapped among the blades feed on the damp within and

126

burst, and of course I wouldn't think of the night before, of any stray cigarettes when I'd heard and then not heard his foot-steps somewhere out by the fence line, which wasn't strange anymore, not for a long time at least, since most nights now he walked out in the dark alone, following old deer trails and dried up vernal streams, his boots when he came back smelling of moss and rain, shirtsleeves and hair studded with burrs, and I knew and I didn't know why, I knew vanishing was just another way to both want and not want to be loved, but we hardly said a word those months we took the horses down the abandoned road, each time dodging our way among ruts, each time hoping they wouldn't throw a shoe against a stone or a wedge of ice, the Belgian in them so far eclipsing the Morgan till they'd gotten big the way mountains are, if mountains had hoofs and could kick, like those times when they broke through the fence and struck straight for the alfalfa fields up the hill, spooking a little when we tried to bring them back, snorting, pulling, shaking their heads, and sometimes one of them sidestepped and for weeks my toes glowed a shifting, grackle-wing blue, but by summer the insurance cleared, by the Fourth the town came back and raised a new barn, strawberry ice cream and lemonade in the shade, the frame pulled up and topped out with an evergreen all in a day, and our father was sunburned and sweat-beaded and happy, the horses' skin shivered with more than just flies, and I knew it wouldn't be long now, I knew there are ways to lose that do not belong to sparks or hay or cigarettes, there are some empty places you can visit but never build from, and who would have known except me and the horses flicking their tails in the grass that the last thing he did in that fresh-built barn was to set free a swallow caught in the loft, was to dangle his legs from the rafters and swing a net till he snagged it, then he placed that bird in my hands like the most or the last fragile thing in the world, the eyes of it darker even than smoke, the shape and the hum of blood in it like nothing else but a heart, and the two of us looked at it just for one breath, hoping our palms hadn't marked it against its brothers before he opened the hay loft door, before he told me to give it a toss but gentler, and then to watch it go.

Erin Calabria grew up in rural Western Massachusetts and currently lives in Magdeburg, Germany. She studied writing at Marlboro College and radio documentary at the Salt Institute in Portland, Maine. Her documentary work has aired on National Public Radio, and her fiction and nonfiction have appeared in *Third Point Press, Atlas and Alice, FIVE:2:ONE* magazine, *100 Word Story*, and in other journals. Her nonfiction essay "Redshift," appearing in *Atlas and Alice*, Issue 3, was nominated for *Best of the Net 2015*.

Nick Admussen :
Parable of the Rotary Phone

[From *Inch*, No. 30, Winter 2016]

I found myself at a summer camp for the scions of upper-middle-crust Houston, Texas. During the day, we alternated between violence and Jesus: archery in the morning, a break for lunch while devotional rock played on the PA, then skeet shooting or lacrosse in the afternoon. Some evenings, we would smear our faces with mud and skulk through the forest to defend or obtain flags; other nights would feature a film about faith, and the older campers would grab and fondle each other ecstatically in the dim light of Christ's love. The hard and soft, shove and tug of our days was meant to come together during the rock-climbing excursion, where we would master the jagged and unfeeling skin of the earth itself in order to experience an early-morning sermon at the pinnacle.

It was explained to me that the guide rope, the one that arrowed straight down the cliff face, was the teaching of Christ. It was straight and the absolute truth. If you climbed along it without deviation, you might fall, but you'd never fall far—your trust in the Lord and your faith community, represented by your belayer, would catch you. If you ignored it, well, the counselor knifed up his shoulders and looked at a spot a few degrees above the horizon as if to say, *in that case I'll be doing something else, because I wouldn't want to be present for your unavoidable and well-deserved suffering.* I made it about three-quarters of the way up before I heard the buzzing: the guideline was laid over a wasp's nest. I went far out to the left to get around it, and when I got to the top, I got a talking-to. As it progressed, I realized that the counselors had been given a powerful injunction against directly saying that any camper's behavior had offended or disappointed Jesus. Being a Christian child, I would normally have been turned into a sobbing wreck by the barest hint that I was responsible for the sufferings on Calvary, but as a fatherless child, I was fixated on proving the existence of the wasp's nest.

At the crest of the sermon on the crest of the hilltop, the camp organizer held up an old rotary telephone. He unscrewed the mouthpiece, detached the wiring inside, took off the face and the little card with the numbers on it, and opened up the base, letting its innards spill out. He put the whole mess into a big Ziploc bag and started shaking it. "Now, some people," he said flatly, "think that if you shake this bag long enough, you're going to get a working telephone by random chance. Does that seem right to you? Look at all this"—with his non-bag-shaking hand he indicated all the Arkansas around us, the white clapboard cross, the trees that kept the riverbank firm and the ones sucking slowly down into the river—"look at yourselves. Does this seem like an accident to you, or does it seem like something that was created for a purpose?" He stopped shaking the bag, but I began to want him to keep shaking it, to shake it harder. I wanted to grab him and shake him until he died and was replaced by someone who was even better at shaking the bag. I didn't care if we got a phone out of it or not. The air was cool; it was that brief part of a hot day where the breeze is light and variable, and the hair on my arms stood up. I felt an invisible set of hands grabbing me by the shoulders, their fingers clenching. I felt my body moving back and forth slowly to the beat of my own pulse.

Nick Admussen is an assistant professor of Chinese literature at Cornell University. He is the author of the scholarly monograph *Recite and Refuse: Contemporary Chinese Prose Poetry* (2016), as well as four chapbooks of poetry, including *Movie Plots* from Epiphany Editions. He has translated the work of Nobel Prize–winner Liu Xiaobo, *samizdat* poet Genzi, and the poetry collection *Floral Mutter* by the Sichuan poet Ya Shi. He holds a PhD from Princeton University, and an MFA in poetry writing from Washington University in St. Louis.

Robert Scotellaro :
What Remains

[From *Bad Motel* (Big Table Publishing, 2016)]

She tells me she saw shadows on the wall. What looked like robots in top hats. She's been hitting the morphine pump pretty good. Says, watching that small TV is like looking at a rock in a snowstorm. And would I tap some salt on her tongue. Those packets. Wants to feel the tang. *Something. Anything other* . . . That tongue that taught English Lit to troubled teens. Hemingway's big fish in ruin. The catcher in that chest high rye, catching. A tongue that wags at nurses flying by. "Now the sugar," she says. Points. Sticks her tongue out at me again.

Robert Scotellaro has published widely in national and international books, journals, and anthologies, including W. W. Norton's *Flash Fiction International, The Best Small Fictions 2016, NANO Fiction, Gargoyle, New Flash Fiction Review*, and many others. He is the author of seven literary chapbooks, several books for children, and three story collections: *Measuring the Distance* (Blue Light Press, 2012); *What We Know So Far* (winner of the 2015 Blue Light Press Book Award); and *Bad Motel* (Big Table Publishing, 2016). He is the recipient of *Zone 3*'s Rainmaker Award in Poetry. Scotellaro, along with James Thomas, is currently editing an anthology of micro fiction forthcoming from W. W. Norton & Company. He lives in San Francisco.

Hannah Harlow :
The Farmers' Market

[From *SmokeLong Quarterly*, Issue Fifty-Three, 2016]

There were booths and stalls selling soaps and granola and candles and jewelry rings bangles earrings necklaces chokers with chunky stones and ropes and beads performers juggling rainbow colored balls or tossing rings that disappeared. I had the boys with me and I told them to stay close and they did they were close the whole time we rounded corners and weaved through the crowd and we found the puppet man and we found the popsicle man and we found the vegetable stall that had our kale and tomatoes and basil for dinner we doubled back and crisscrossed and I kept seeing this boy not my boy but definitely the same boy and he always seemed to be alone. Finally I stopped across the way and people passed between us and my boys sucked at their popsicles they didn't ask questions they didn't see him did anyone else see him? He looked maybe five or maybe older if he was small for his age he looked all around him but not like he was looking for someone or like he was lost but also not like he was curious or like he knew what he was doing there. I told my boys to stick close again harsher than I meant to and they followed as I crossed the expanse between us getting clipped by an overlarge pocketbook and nearly trampled by a mess of kids possibly all belonging to the same family and I wondered as I always wonder how do you do it. When we reached him I knelt and my boys were on either side of me and we were all the same height and for a moment it was quiet we were in our own little bubble and he didn't seem scared at all so I thought maybe I was wrong maybe he was all right. Are you here with your mom or dad I said and he just stared at me my name is Sasha I said and these are my kids Antonio and Micah and he just stared at us my boys were staring too and I felt bad I didn't have a popsicle to give the boy. Who are you here with I tried again he shrugged and I looked down trying to think what to say and then I saw blood smeared on his shin on his ankle or maybe it was just dirt. Are you hurt I asked and his eyes widened now he was paying attention and I realized my mistake that you have to come at little boys from the side. No no I said what's your name but it was too many questions it was too late he didn't say anything. He never said anything. We just moved here I said I thought maybe I would just talk awhile and maybe hit on a subject that would get him talking get him talking the way my boys sometimes talked and couldn't stop. We don't know too many people I said Antonio just started school he has Miss Caderra in room 202 what about you. But he didn't answer and Antonio hung on to my shirt like he wished I would stop like duh ma we don't know him no one knows him but Antonio has always been cautious. These popsicles are pretty good they're made out of lime and what else I said to my boys and Micah yelled booberries but they weren't blueberries they were huckleberries or maybe just strawberries big chunks of them I'll buy you one I said and the boy ran away so fast and around a vendor's stall and into a crowd I lost sight of him. I stood up because my knees and the scar from my C-section ached even though it had been four years some people say it never goes away. I found a police officer and told him about the boy he looked around like he might be able to find him without moving at all he nodded he said he'd keep an eye out he said thank you, thank you for caring, or maybe I just imagined that last part. Micah complained he was hungry Antonio complained he was hungry we left the police officer we all held hands and found the car. Before they were born I never would have noticed that little boy and sometimes now when I ask Micah and Antonio how their days were or what they did in school and they say I don't remember I want to shake them are you okay are you okay just answer me but instead I say it's okay try harder tomorrow.

Hannah Harlow earned an MFA in fiction from the Bennington Writing Seminars. Her flash fiction has appeared in *SmokeLong Quarterly, The Stoneslide Corrective, Synaesthesia Magazine, Quick Fiction, failbetter,* and elsewhere. Some of her longer fiction has been published in *Vol. One Brooklyn, Day One,* and *Animal.* In early 2017, she completed a residency at the Studios at MASS MoCA. By day she works in publishing. Harlow lives with her family on a horseless horse farm north of Boston.

Kimberly King Parsons
In Our Circle

[From *NANO Fiction*, Vol. 10, 2016]

If she was afraid of us, she never let on. She'd pull her chair right into our bloody-minded circle, get dirty up to her wrists. It didn't matter if we pinched pots or rolled out dicks and balls, at the end of each class the art shrink would take whatever we'd made and mash it all back in on itself. We'd watch her small hands choke through the mess and try not to levitate the craft table with our peckers.

"It's a process," she told us.

Of course there would be threats and thrown elbows, sometimes somebody getting grabbed by the throat for what seemed like nothing at all. When this happened the art shrink would sigh and push the call button. The doctors would rush in, their little clipboards up like shields. The rest of us sat still, hands soft where everyone could see.

"Allow these distractions to deepen your concentration," the art shrink said.

When they let me out I was just as mad as when I went in, only fatter and too lazy to exercise my wrath. Plus, I'd shaved my eyebrows off for no real reason and what grew back was fine and blond and seemed to endear the world to me. I'd done the work and passed their tests, but my mind was still snarled.

To keep the red thoughts away, I bought myself a card table, a couple tubs of modeling clay. Now I make little ball-people and smoosh them down. A thousand snakes, warped pancakes. I think about the art shrink, how she told a roomful of monsters to leave space for luminous moments. I squish that thick stuff around, contemplate my talents, wonder if this is what she meant.

Kimberly King Parsons's writing has appeared in *New South, Black Warrior Review, No Tokens, Bookforum,* and elsewhere. She earned an MFA in fiction from Columbia University, where she served as the editor-in-chief of *Columbia: A Journal of Literature and Art.* She received the 2016 *Indiana Review* Fiction Prize and placed second in the 2017 *Joyland* Open Border Fiction Prize. One of her stories, "Fiddlebacks," was recently featured on the *Ploughshares* blog "The Best Short Story I Read in a Lit Mag This Week." She lives in Portland, Oregon.

Amy Sayre Baptista
Pike County Feminism

[From *Corium*, Summer 2016]

The night we catch a Brown Thrush in her twig trap, Aunt Gin says, "Mama cows eat their afterbirth to protect their young."

"From predators?" I ask.

"The same," she says. "You won't lay in long grass but a twitch for you see a coyote or bob cat ambling by. I put my money on a horned cow every time against a coyote."

She holds the delicate bird to her lips, but doesn't bite. Looks me in the eye. "Everything you catch is not yours to keep. That's what separates us from them." She says mama cows signal their young to stay. Positioning a calf in the tall grass, hidden, not to attract attention of enemies she cannot fight off in her absence to drink or eat. Stillness is safety. Calves do not question the wisdom of cows. Don't know to move against their mama's advice.

Aunt Gin says, "It's why baby deer get wound up in hay rakes or tangled in combines. Babies don't know to run."

I repeat that. Babies don't know to run. And start to cry.

She opens her palms and the thrush flies.

"When your mama left," Aunt Gin says, "she didn't know what was coming."

She looks up and shields her eyes with one hand, watching a thunderhead's slow roll eastward. "Nobody knows what's coming. Just like a doe cannot imagine a tractor, cannot imagine the breaking power of an iron machine on a fawn's dappled hide."

She brushes a gnarled finger against the bruise shadowing my left eye.

"You only trust the long grass up to a point, child." She takes my hand in hers and examines my palm. "I knew bad men to go blind from a child's suffering." Tracing a line in the center, she says, "Retribution comes."

In the next trap, we find a Blue Jay. She tells me the males have the pretty colors, then quick-twists his neck. She jerks out three azure tail feathers and braids them into my hair.

"In this life," Aunt Gin says, "we build our own traps, build our own wings."

She tosses the still warm carcass into the grass and brushes her hands against her skirt. She holds her hand out to me. "Mamas are always saying, be careful. Mine said it to me. Yours said it to you. Be careful out a mama's mouth don't mean nothing 'cept protect yourself better than I did."

Amy Sayre Baptista's writing has appeared in *Corium, SmokeLong Quarterly, Ninth Letter, The Butter, Alaska Quarterly Review,* and other journals. She was a SAFTA fellow (2015), a CantoMundo Poetry fellow (2013), and a scholarship recipient to the Disquiet Literary Festival in Lisbon, Portugal (2011). She performs with Kale Soup for the Soul, a Portuguese-American artist's collective, and Poetry While You Wait. She is a cofounder of Plates&Poetry, a community arts program focused on food and writing. She has an MFA in Fiction from the University of Illinois, Urbana–Champaign, and teaches humanities at Western Governors University. She lives in Chicago, Illinois.

Michael C. Smith :
Bass Weather

[From *Gemini Magazine*, May 2016]

I was having no luck with the bass and was wondering if I'd ever have any luck with the bass when a woman wearing a black strapless gown and a string of pearls showed up with her two boys.

The kids had bamboo poles, the wrong gear in my opinion, and she was holding her high-heeled shoes in one hand and a beer in the other as she picked her way among the creek stones. She wore a lot of lipstick but it looked good on her when she smiled at me just before she took a pull on the Pabst Blue Ribbon. The boys struggled with hooks, worms, bobbers, and sinkers but they looked grateful to be there and didn't whine or complain. No wonder: she actually helped bait their hooks, her long red nails precise in the way they pincered the protesting worms.

Every now and again I'd look over and she'd look back and smile, until I broke the ice: "Good bass weather," I said.

"Yes," she agreed. "Just what I was thinking."

But she didn't ask if I was having any luck, a sure sign she was just putting me on. "You weren't thinking that," I said. "You're an imposter."

"Yes," she said. "I'm not a meteorologist."

"Just what I thought. If you don't mind my asking. . . ."

"A funeral," she said. "My dear, dear half-sister."

"I see."

"No, you don't. Do you ever see? You're such an idiot."

"This is a good start," I said. "Got any more beer?"

"Of course." She widened the mouth of her large purse, revealing much more than a six pack.

"How much you got in there?" I asked.

"Case. Case and a half. Do you think that's enough?"

"That should be entirely adequate," I said.

The day bore on. The boys weren't having any luck with the bass either, and we had finished off the Pabst. Turned out her husband—who was her second husband—owned a gas station, and he always worked there—sixteen–nineteen hours a day. Day in. Day out. Work, work, work. Her half-sister had died an agonizing death of leukemia, and the woman had dressed to go to the funeral, but her husband wouldn't take a day off to watch the kids and only let her know at the last minute. So she figured she might as well do something they wanted to do and didn't give a hoot about her outfit.

"You would have been one of the better dressed among the mourners," I said.

"Thank you," she said. "That helps."

The boys rarely said anything to us, just sometimes asking for permission to go pee in the bushes or for a drink of water.

"Nice kids," I said at one of the many junctures.

"Yes, I am blessed," she said. "Truly blessed, as though there is any other way of being blessed. Did you ever hear such a crock? Don't you hate people who make more of what is already too much?"

"I've only hated one person like that," I said. "An English teacher who used to say 'This is literature; this is life' over and over until we students started hating both."

"That's power," she said.

"It sure is."

She suddenly looked at me as though I had said something that meant something to her. She touched my hand. I was frightened: images from Chinese New Years past seized some of my senses. I swallowed with great deliberation.

She said, "When I was seven I wanted a doll that looked just like anyone I knew."

"Like who?"

"Just anyone. My stupid sister would have been fine. The girl in my class who squeaked quietly throughout grade school. I didn't care. Just anyone, you understand, anyone that didn't look like a doll."

"Normal eyes?" I offered.

"Right. Normal eyes, lips, regular chin. No big deal. Except you know what? 'No can do, Jim.' That's what my mother said. 'No can do.'"

"Who's Jim?"

"I don't know. She just always added that name to 'No can do.'"

I needed to find us a way out of her fun-house recollections.

"And?" I said.

"Exactly. And?"

"Yeah, huh?"

"Right."

We had entered the valley of monosyllabic utterances, and it was nice there and peaceful until one of the boys started yelling and heaving on his bamboo pole. We rose and staggered over to the edge of the creek bank. I thought maybe it was a tire or a log, the way the pole was bending, but there was something definitely struggling at the end of the line. The other boy grabbed the pole to help and then I grabbed it as well as their mother, and the tip of the pole was bent almost to the water, and something was thrashing down there, something dark and dense and angry, something bigger than all of us. On the count of three, we all tugged at the same time and out of the water flew her husband, who landed on the matt grass smelling of gasoline and flapping like an idiot.

I went ahead and introduced myself but it seemed lost on him, and, to tell you the truth, also lost on the woman and the boys, who gathered Dad up and helped him flop home, leaving me with the rest of the worms and a good case of the empties.

Michael C. Smith is the author of *Writing Dangerous Poetry* (McGraw-Hill) and coauthor of *Everyday Creative Writing: Panning for Gold in the Kitchen Sink* (McGraw-Hill). His work has appeared in *Gemini Magazine, The Iowa Review, Seneca Review, Northwest Review,* and *Atlanta Review,* among others. A graduate of the MFA program at the University of Arizona, he teaches writing at Copper Mountain Community College, Joshua Tree, California.

Julia Slavin
Groundbreaker

[From *Subtropics*, Issue 22, 2016]

Judy from across the street had a psychedelic bus with broken windows parked in her driveway. She said it belonged to her daughter and that if her daughter ever moved out, Judy would move to the Florida Keys with nothing but a postbox. About my husband's Hummer H1 she said, "What's with that boat in your driveway?" I had never complained about the bus.

She fell in her driveway and cracked open her head one day. At first I thought her screams were coming from a fox. But then I realized they were human. I did what I was taught at the Red Cross. I kept her talking, I called 911, I got a blanket. I took her to George Washington Hospital. It was five o'clock, the shitfaced shift. The ER was filled with prisoners.

The H1 is gone, the psychedelic bus is gone. The daughter is still there with a boyfriend who shoves her against metal trash cans. I have called the police many times. I'm walking the dogs by Judy's house and she's cutting her feather reed. I say how sad I am to see it go, and head to the trail with the dogs. When I pass her on the way home, she's waiting. She says, "Just what are you trying to tell me?"

When I'm anxious, I spit when I talk. I say I'm sorry to see the seasons change. That's a lie, because her grasses never turn green and the seeds fly and land in my garden and I have to dig the roots out of my garden with a groundbreaker. I lie again about the splendor of autumn. I spit and make the mistake of saying *ethereal* when I mean *ephemeral.*

Julia Slavin is the author of the story collection *The Woman Who Cut off Her Leg at the Maidstone Club* (Henry Holt, 1999) and the novel *Carnivore Diet* (W. W. Norton, 2006). She is the winner of a Rona Jaffe Foundation Writers' Award, *GQ*'s Frederick Exley Award for Short Fiction, and a Pushcart Prize. Alec Baldwin read her story "Covered" as part of the Symphony Space Selected Shorts Series. Her stories have appeared in *McSweeney's, Tin House, Subtropics, Mississippi Review, Salmagundi, The Best of Tin House,* and the *Tin House* publication *Fantastic Women: 18 Tales of the Surreal and Sublime.*

Sherrie Flick :
Boiled Clear

[From *Whiskey, Etc.: Short (Short) Stories* (Queens Ferry
Press, 2016)]

Suzy quickly sliced the Brussels sprouts, shredding them
thinly across the cutting board until she had a tangled mess of
light green ribbon. She split the garlic, chopped it. The pan on
medium flame, the olive oil sizzling. Suzy toasted pecans. She
browned the tofu.

Later all of this would seem foolish. Making dinner for a
dead man. But as the smell lingered in the her kitchen, as she
took the stairs up to her bedroom, drunk with drinking wine
for two, she wouldn't think of fools. The snuffed candles and
their sulfur smell would follow her under the covers where
she'd think of resolution.

Suzy cooked the dinner. Set the table. Waited, hands
folded. And then, with a cookbook open, considered the other
recipes she might have chosen. Better recipes. More appro-
priate dishes. She decided to chop some apples and throw
together a quick cobbler. Easier than worrying or thinking
about Neil standing her up again.

Instead Neil was on a highway driving his pickup too fast,
not wearing his seatbelt because the seatbelts didn't work in his
piece of shit truck. He would've been drumming his fingers on

the sill of the open window. He'd have wiggled the tuner to get the game on, run a hand through his hair, maybe wondered what he was doing, heading toward Suzy again. No one would ever know, of course, where he was headed that night. She'd certainly called to confirm. They'd flirted like they did sometimes on the phone. Neil had said, Sure, sure he remembered. He'd pick up some ice cream, even, because she was sweet.

No ice cream in the truck. Suzy had asked the police officer on the phone. Not that they'd known to call her or have a reason to. She found things out days later. After she'd eaten the crispy-cold meal. The browned sprouts, the sweet pecans, the tofu—all shriveled over rice. She'd forked it slowly—holding out even at the end. And still, Suzy had saved a little container for him, hating herself.

Neil didn't set an anchor. He came and went—but mostly went. When he did come he was either all-on happy love or moody as shit, gliding like a ghost from room to room. Suzy couldn't figure. Some days she couldn't tell if he even liked her or if she liked him. Other days, everything boiled clear and passionate. Boom. And they were off. Hot and sizzling. All this smashed between silences and days apart.

Neil had been driving south. A tire blew out from what they could tell, and then he maybe hit some kind of oily patch. Suzy was sure that he'd thought no problem, knew he could handle it. Until the end. The police officer said he didn't feel any pain, but they always say that—especially to sometimes-girlfriends sobbing on the other end of the phone. And Suzy didn't know how she felt about the pain. Maybe she wanted Neil to have some, just a few seconds of it.

Suzy had opened the wine. A nice Syrah. She'd checked to see if she had whiskey, in case he didn't want wine. He never wanted wine. She didn't know if he liked wine, but she did and even though it was Neil's birthday celebration, she wanted some things for herself. This was the problem, Suzy told herself later on: she was selfish at the wrong moments.

Suzy washed all the dishes before Neil should have arrived so he couldn't offer. So she wouldn't know if he would or he wouldn't. Everything neat and humming in the dishwasher. The kitchen looking homey and warm. Candles. Linen napkins. She knew this wasn't the kind of birthday celebration Neil wanted. She knew a mistake when she saw one. But Suzy couldn't help herself with these kinds of kindnesses. She wanted to show people their own potential—show them what the world could be like when they weren't driving around work sites in crappy pickup trucks, eating fried food, tossing the wrappers under the seat. She wanted to civilize Neil. And maybe, she thought in later years, that was precisely why he was driving so fast—to spite her and her fancy tofu meal. To show her.

She dreamed up some other things because she could: he'd had a change of clothes in the back of the truck. Nice jeans and a shirt he planned to wear. That he'd started dialing her phone but then stopped, knowing he'd be on time for once. She imagined that he'd planned to talk about moving in together, buying a new truck. She invented these things, and they made her feel better.

That night, before she turned everything off, before she gave up for good—long into the night, really, if she had to admit it, she stepped out onto the front porch. City sounds nearby, the sliver of a moon, and she felt her life turning for the better—like fresh earth dug up and flipped over.

Sherrie Flick is the author of the novel *Reconsidering Happiness*, the chapbook *I Call This Flirting*, and the story collection *Whiskey, Etc.*, a finalist for a Foreword INDIES Best Book of the Year award. Her fiction has appeared in many anthologies and journals, including W. W. Norton's *Flash Fiction Forward* and *New Sudden Fiction*, *Ploughshares*, and *SmokeLong Quarterly*. She has received fellowships from Pennsylvania Council on the Arts, Sewanee Writers' Conference, Ucross, and Atlantic Center for the Arts. She teaches at Chatham University and serves as codirector for the Chautauqua Writers' Festival. A new story collection is forthcoming from Autumn House Press in Fall 2018.

Rebecca Schiff :
What We Bought

[From *Wigleaf*, April 10, 2016]

He bought me flowers and a vase. He gave me the vase three days after he gave me the flowers. I don't know what he thought would happen in the interim, maybe that I would just leave the flowers on the table, and the flowers would die there. He wrote "Don't forget to trim the stems!" so I guess he thought I would put the flowers in something, like a jar, which I did do, but the jar was not tall enough for the flowers, even after I trimmed the stems, so I had to go out and buy my own vase.

I bought the vase at a complicated store that also sold chrysanthemums and soap. The woman who owned the store tried to show me a vase that cost more than a hundred dollars, a heavy vase with flowers embossed on the glass. For a minute, I thought I needed a vase that cost more than a hundred dollars. Then I asked the woman if she had anything else. She started removing flowers from a cheaper vase. Maybe she had never sold a vase before.

By the time I got the vase from him, I already had a vase. It only cost twelve dollars. I don't know how much his vase cost, but somewhere between twelve and a hundred. I'm going to guess forty. Later, I gave the vase he bought me to my aunt.

"This will look good in your dining room," I told her. "Take it. I can't look at it anymore."

My aunt loved that I couldn't look at a vase a man had given me. Giving her my vase made it seem like gifts from men happened to me all the time, or at least often enough that I would know what to do with one. I had gotten other gifts from other men: a parasol, a record, a box of tea. Those times, I had set the gifts down in the vestibule of my building until someone took them away. The parasol and the record went fast. The tea nobody would take. I watched it sit in the vestibule of my building, next to the mailboxes, day after day. Finally I brought the tea back upstairs to my apartment and threw it in the garbage.

My aunt told her dinner guests the story of the vase the night she got it, then told the story again a few more times before the vase and the story of the vase stopped being new to her.

Rebecca Schiff is the author of the short story collection *The Bed Moved* (Knopf, 2016), a finalist for the Art Seidenbaum Award for First Fiction. Her short stories have appeared in *n+1, Electric Literature, The American Reader, Catapult, Guernica, The Guardian, Lenny Letter,* and *Wigleaf*. She graduated from Columbia University's MFA program, where she received a Henfield Prize. She lives in Oregon.

Brian Doyle :
My Devils

[From *The Sun*, Issue 481, January 2016]

One time when I was seven years old, my aunt placed her hands upon me and tried to drive out my devils. I was not aware that I had any resident devils and said so, hesitantly, as she was a firm woman. She said, *You certainly* do *have devils, and they are beginning to manifest.* I did not know what *manifest* meant but did not say so. She moved her hands from my head to my shoulders to my chest and then back up to my head again. I wanted to ask where the devils lived and how many there were and what they looked like and did they know Lucifer personally and was he a decent guy who just snapped one day or what, but she was intent and her eyes were closed and she was not a woman to be interrupted while she was working.

After a while she opened her eyes, and I asked if the devils were gone, and she said, *We will see, we will see.* Even then I knew that if someone said something twice it meant that they were not sure it was so. I was learning that a lot of times what people meant was not at all what they said. *Maybe* meant no, and *The Lord will provide* meant the Lord had not yet provided, and *Take your time* meant hurry up. It was hard to learn all the languages spoken in our house. There was the loose limber American language that we all spoke, and then there was the

154

riverine sinuous Irish language that the old people spoke when they were angry, and then there was the chittery sparrowish female language that my mother and grandmother and aunts and the neighborhood women spoke, and then there was the raffish chaffing language that other dads spoke to my dad when they came over for cocktail parties, and then there was the high slow language we all spoke when priests were in the house, and then there were the dialects spoken by only one person—for example, my sister, who spoke the haughty languorous language of her many cats, or my youngest brother, Tommy, who spoke Tommy, which only he and my sister could understand. She would often translate for him; apparently he talked mostly about cheese and crayons.

The rest of that day I went around feeling filled with devils and slightly queasy about it. I figured they must be living in my stomach or lungs, because those were the only places inside me with any air to breathe. I asked my oldest brother if devils needed air, the way people do, and he made a gesture with his hand that meant *Go away right now.* Hand gestures were another language in our family, and our mother was the most eloquent speaker of that tongue. If she turned her hand one way it meant *Go get my cigarettes.* If she turned it another way it meant *What you just said is so silly that I am not going to bother to disabuse you of your idiocy.* Still other gestures meant *Whatever*, and *In a thousand years it will all be the same*, and *Take your youngest brother with you and do not attempt to give me lip about it.*

I waited until bedtime to ask my mother about my devils. She was about to make the hand gesture that meant *We will talk about this some other time,* but then she saw my worried expression, and she stopped and sat down with me, and I explained about my aunt and the laying on of hands. My mother made a few incomprehensible sounds in her throat and then talked about her sister as if she were a tree that we were examining from various angles. Her sweet sister was a wonderfully devout person, she said, and she had the very best of intentions, and she had the truest heart of anyone you could ever meet, and she was more alert to the prevalence of miracles than anyone else my mother knew, and you had to admire the depth of her faith—we should all be as committed and dedicated and passionate as she was—but the fact was that we were not quite as committed as my aunt to the more remote possibilities, such as the laying on of hands to dispel demons. *Do you have the slightest idea what I am saying to you?* she asked. I said I did not, hesitantly, because I didn't want her to stop talking so beautifully and entertainingly, and she put her hand on my forehead and said that she loved me, and that it was bedtime, so I'd better hop to it, which I did. As she left, she made a gesture with her hand that meant *If you don't brush your teeth and then try to pretend that you did, I will know you are telling a lie and it will not end well*, and she laughed, and I laughed, and I brushed my teeth.

Brian Doyle (1956–2017) was the editor of *Portland Magazine* at the University of Portland, Oregon. He authored six collections of essays, two nonfiction books, two collections of "proems," a story collection, and several novels including the acclaimed *Mink River*. Doyle's essays, which have appeared in prestigious journals and magazines around the world (*The Atlantic Monthly, Harper's, Orion, The American Scholar,* the *New York Times*, the *Times of London*) have been reprinted in *Best American Essays, Best American Science and Nature Writing,* and *Best American Spiritual Writing*. Among various honors for his work is a Catholic Book Award, three Pushcart Prizes, the John Burroughs Award for Nature Essays, the 2008 Award in Literature from the American Academy of Arts and Letters, and the 2017 John Burroughs Medal for Distinguished Nature Writing for his novel *Martin Marten*, only the second work of fiction to be awarded the medal in its 90-year history.

Best Small Fictions Finalists

Melanie Boeckmann : Banana Slugs (*StoryShack*)

Owen Booth : The Ultimate Fate of the Universe (*3:AM magazine*)

Kristy Bowen : from Songs for Dead Girls (*Paper Darts*)

Emily Bowers : 698 (*Nanoism*)

Holly Brickley : The More Missed (*matchbook* lit mag)

Raelee Chapman : Golden Girl (*Mascara Review*)

Kim Chinquee : Highball (*Five Points*)

Joanna Penn Cooper : How Not to Read Richard Scarry's Busy, Busy Town at the End of a Long Day (*The Virginia Normal*)

Elaine Cosgrove : Filament (*The Stinging Fly*)

Leesa Cross-Smith : Low, Small (*Blue Fifth Review: Blue Five Notebook Series*)

Christopher DeWan : The 100th Floor (from *Hoopty Time Machines*, Atticus Books)

Stephanie E. Dickinson : Emily and the Dynamite (*West Marin Review*)

Linh Dinh : Travel Tips (*Monkey Business International*)

Zachary Doss : Cold Fish (*Juked*)

Jeff Fearnside : Nuclear Toughskins (from *Making Love While Levitating Three Feet in the Air*, SFASU Press)

Harrison Candelaria Fletcher : Dawn (*Eleven Eleven*)

Sherrie Flick : You Have a Car (from *Whiskey, Etc.*, Queen's Ferry Press)

Richard Garcia : Waking Up (from *Porridge*, Press 53)

Megan Giddings : Again and Again and Again (*Threadcount*)

Dan Gilmore : Hackmuth's Mannequin Dream (from *New Shoes*, KYSO Flash Press)

torrin a. greathouse : not gay as in happy . . . (*Calamus Journal*)

Lydia Copeland Gwyn : The Day Is Full of Wheat Stalks . . . (*New World Writing*)

Julianna Holland : White Matter (Bath Flash Fiction Award)

Ingrid Jendrzejewski : Roll and Curl (Bath Flash Fiction Award)

Shane Jones : Gazebo (*The Conium Review*)

Patrick Kelling : Consumption (*SAND Journal*)

Carmen Lau : Inside the Wolf (from *The Girl Wakes*, Alternating Current Press)

Michael Martone : The Incinerator (from *Memoranda*, Bull City Press)

Bobbie Ann Mason : The Whirling Circle (*Great Jones Street*)

Rupprecht Mayer : Chores [Christopher Allen, translator] (*SmokeLong Quarterly*)

rob mclennan : The city is uneven (*PRISM international*)

Frankie McMillan : The world has become bigger than my head can ever hold (from *My Mother and the Hungarians*, Canterbury UP)

Shivani Mehta : the invisible girl and the curiosity of strangers (*New Flash Fiction Review*)

Christopher Merkner : Human Contact Near Philadelphia, 2012–2014 (*Hayden's Ferry Review*)

Elena Murphy : Pebbles and Water (*Calamus Journal*)

Henry Peplow : Zeus Falls to Earth (*Ad Hoc Fiction*)

Patrick Pink : Take My Boyfriend to His Tangihanga (*Flash Frontier: An Adventure in Flash Fiction*)

Meg Pokrass : Elizabeths (from *The Dog Looks Happy Upside Down*, Etruscan Press)

Spencer David Potts : Lift (*Hypertrophic Press*)

Ian Seed : Being True (from *Identity Papers*, Shearsman Books)

Angela Sorby : No One Knows Where the Ladder Goes (Blue Cubicle Press)

Julia Strayer : In the Shape of a Small Bird (*Fiction Southeast*)

Laura Tansley : The Wake She Leaves Like a Whirlpool (from *Nothing to Declare: A Guide to the Flash Sequence*, White Pine Press)

Ben Tanzer : The Look of Love, Take Two (from *Sex*, Sunnyoutside Press)

Cathy Ulrich : The Magician's Affair (*Monkeybicycle*)

Deb Olin Unferth : Draft (*Wigleaf*)

James Valvis : Boxes (*Juked*)

Anne Elizabeth Weisgerber : Upfurler (Pure Slush Books)

Theresa Wyatt : Gettysburg, July, 1863 (*Prime Number Magazine*)

Spotlight on *SmokeLong Quarterly*

Best Small Fictions : Give us a brief summation of the history of *SmokeLong Quarterly*.

Christopher Allen, Managing Editor : *SLQ* will be 15 years old soon! In online-journal years, that's around 150. Founded by Dave Clapper in 2003, *SmokeLong* got its name from the Chinese expression for how long it takes to read a piece of very short fiction. And wouldn't reading a brief, killer story be a great smoking cure? The story instead of the cigarette? Imagine a world of people jonesing for their story breaks.

SLQ has been edited and guest edited by most of the important voices in flash, including Randall Brown, Beth Thomas, and Tara Laskowski, along with Kathy Fish, the namesake of *SLQ*'s Kathy Fish Fellowship. We've grown to an army of 16 dedicated and diverse editors led by Tara Laskowski, and we publish weekly now as well as quarterly. On top of this, there's always something interesting up on the *SLQ* blog relevant to flash fiction.

BSF : Congratulations on two winners (Hannah Harlow, "The Farmers' Market," and Cole Meyer, "Nightstands") and a finalist. Each year you have been well represented not just on our Best Of list, but on others. What do you think accounts for the success of *SLQ* in general, and of these two very different winners in particular?

CA : Thank you! We are thrilled for Hannah Harlow and Cole Meyer. In terms of technique, Harlow's story boldly sets its own rules of syntax and what constitutes a unit of thought in a stream-of-consciousness narrative. It also nails voice and mood and makes your heart beat faster. It's a homerun of a story. In "Nightstands" Meyer starts with a great idea, a play on words, and unravels his character's dilemma with precision and brevity. The success of *SLQ* depends greatly on writers who send us stories like these.

Having the continuity of dedicated editors at the helm has also contributed immensely to our longevity, but the key to *SLQ*'s success is the team. By the time a quarterly issue is published, around 70 people have been involved: artists, interviewers, guest readers, staff readers, blog and social media editors, and of course writers. That's a lot of people and a lot of love for flash fiction.

BSF : Are you working on anything new at *SmokeLong* that relates to the future of flash fiction?

CA : So happy you asked! Yes, we are always thinking of ways to shape the future of flash. In 2016 we launched *SLQ*'s Global Flash Series, which features non-Anglo stories in their original language accompanied by the English translation. And what a boost it is for us that the first story in this series [Rupprecht Mayer, "Chores"] was a finalist for *The Best Small Fictions*. Currently, we're open to French and German submissions on a rolling basis. Upcoming languages include Swahili and Hebrew. Since *SLQ* embraces diversity—you might even say we bear hug it—it just seems natural for us to stretch beyond English to discover what other languages do with this tight space of flash.

Spotlight on Joy Williams

Best Small Fictions : We are thrilled to have one of our greatest writers included in this volume. Congratulations on the success of *Ninety-Nine Stories of God*! It was a *New York Times* Notable Book and named as a Best Book of the Year by many prestigious journals and magazines such as *Esquire* and *Publishers Weekly*. Given its overall theme, can you tell us how the book as a whole was conceived? And what drove you to explore these modern parables in short vignettes?

Joy Williams : The idea came from Thomas Bernhard's unsettling *The Voice Imitator*, but he was a secular sort of guy and I was more interested in glimpsing God's mysterious movements among us. Though actually, I probably didn't think of it that way at the beginning. I was just having a terrible, terrible time with a novel I was writing . . . and still am. My agent, Amanda Urban, said, Well, Joy, some of these aren't as good as others, you know . . . why don't you do *Ninety-Two Stories of God*?

BSF : You once wrote that the "writer must not really know what he is knowing, what he is learning to know when he writes, which is more than the knowing of it." We had a hard time narrowing the many wonderful works in the collection down to the two ("Dearest" and "Polyurethane") that made the finalist list. But what unites them both are the complete, dense worlds and complex emotions you depicted in a small space, and the unexpected and powerful endings. The final lines are small gavels knocking you into awareness in some way. Did you write these two fictions knowing where you were going, or did you follow your own advice and did the writing tell you what you needed to know?

JW : Thank you. "Polyurethane" always seemed a little long to me but there was that wonderful Catlin quote. I travel a lot and stay in many uneven places but I always harbor the hope that someone will have left a small message behind in beautiful penmanship. An enlightening message, of course! Plus I very much like the word *glebe*. As for "Dearest," that concerned someone I knew rather well though the house wasn't set alight. All the stories in *Ninety-Nine* were gifts brought by different messengers.

BSF : If you could give one piece of advice to new writers learning to write "small," what would it be?

JW : So many times in a single day we glimpse a view beyond the apparent. Write those moments down. They might not speak to you at first. But eventually they might. Everybody writes too long and too much anyway, sacrificing significance for story. Truth be told, we all want to be poets.

About the Series Editor

Amy Hempel is the author of four acclaimed story collections. They were compiled and published in 2006 as *The Collected Stories*, which was named one of the Ten Best Books of the year by the *New York Times* and won the Ambassador Book Award for best fiction of the year. She is the recipient of fellowships from the Guggenheim Foundation and the USA Foundation, and won the Rea Award and PEN/Malamud Award, among others. In 2015, Hempel received the John William Corrington Award for Literary Excellence from Centenary College. Her work has been translated into more than twenty languages, and her stories have been heavily anthologized, including in *Best American Short Stories*; *Best American Nonrequired Reading*; *Life Is Short—Art Is Shorter: In Praise of Brevity* (eds. Shields and Cooperman); and *Flash Fiction Forward: 80 Very Short Stories* (eds. Shapard and Thomas). A member of both the American Academy of Arts and Letters and the American Academy of Arts and Sciences, Hempel taught at Harvard, New York University, Sarah Lawrence, Bennington, and elsewhere, and now teaches at the University of Florida.

Reissue
from Braddock Avenue Books

October 2017

Reissue
from Braddock Avenue Books

THE BEST
SMALL FICTIONS
2016

Guest Editor
STUART
DYBEK

Series Editor
Tara L. Masih

October 2017

CPSIA information can be obtained
at www.ICGtesting.com
Printed in the USA
FSOW02n0445081017
39420FS

9 780998 966717